PRICELESS

A TROPICAL AUTHORS NOVELLA

DEBORAH BROWN   NICHOLAS HARVEY   DON RICH

DOWN ISLAND
PUBLISHING

Printed in the United States of America

First Printing, 2023

ISBN-13: 978-1-956026-52-8

Cover design: Harvey Books, LLC

Editor: Gretchen Tannert Douglas

1

Grand Cayman

Nora Sommer eased her tall, lean body through the opening, careful not to drag her scuba tank against the rusting metal of the shipwreck. Playing the beam of her underwater flashlight around the pitch-black room, she watched small fish flit away and hide behind the large marine transmissions which appeared to hang from one wall among a myriad of pipes and other machinery.

The USS *Kittiwake* had sat upright on the sandy seafloor for almost seven years before Tropical Storm Nate had rolled her onto her side and pushed the artificial reef up against a nearby coral bommie. Now, once inside the 251-foot-long wreck, a diver could easily become disoriented by a world tipped over.

A second beam of light joined Nora's as her friend and dive buddy, AJ Bailey, entered the engine room. A dozen years older than Nora, AJ owned her own business on the island, Mermaid Divers, and was more like a big sister than simply a friend. The two experienced divers finned gently around the cramped space, careful not to disturb the fine layer of silt accumulated over every surface.

Movement to her right caught Nora's attention, and she redirected her flashlight, only to catch a small cloud of grayish-brown haze wafting through the water where something had been just moments before. Most likely it had been one of the many squirrelfish, grunts, or even a small grouper, but the young off-duty police constable felt a tingle of caution.

With nothing visible beyond the circular beams captured by their lights, Nora constantly felt like she was looking down a narrow tunnel surrounded by darkness. Many a diver had succumbed to the claustrophobia and isolated feeling of being deep inside a sunken ship, but not Nora; she thrived on the tension. With a combination of her Norwegian upbringing and the tragedies she'd endured during the past few years, the twenty-year-old was stoic and determined. Her heart rate remained low, and her movements were precise, yet relaxed.

During the day, light penetrated the wreck through a series of hatches, doorways, and cutouts laid open before the artificial reef had been sunk. But at night, the entire ship was shrouded in darkness, inside and out.

She felt the water stir to her left as AJ moved alongside, directing her flashlight between the rusted steel hulks of the transmissions. Nora focused on the deeper side of the room, knowing beyond the hull lay the seafloor where the big ship had nestled firmly into the sand. Her beam caught a willowy flutter of color as something dodged below a series of pipes. Slipping the sling spear from the waistband of her buoyancy control device—or BCD as it was usually called—Nora exhaled the air from her lungs in a stream of bubbles and dropped below the warren of pipes.

Just as her light found the fish she was hunting, something larger slid by her face. Resisting the urge to bolt, she remained perfectly still until the movement in the water subsided. Instinct urged her to move the light away from her target, knowing a larger predator was lurking close by, but Nora forced her focus to remain on her prey.

Slowly, she drew back the spear on the rubber propulsion band. The lionfish before her was the biggest she'd ever seen, its array of scarlet and white fins waving softly as the water stirred around them. Venomous spines seemed to emanate from every angle of the fish's striped body. Using small changes in breath to adjust her buoyancy and subtle fin movements to guide her path, she eased the three-pronged tip of the spear to within a foot of the invasive fish. Silt billowed as she released the spear and her prey tried to bolt. A dull thud let Nora know her needle-sharp tips had hit metal, but the violent writhing on the end of the fiberglass spear told her she'd hit her target.

Lost in a cloud of silt and debris, she pressed the spear against the ship's hull, pinning the lionfish in place. If she tried to draw the spear back, the fish would wrench itself from the tips and be gone in a flash, hiding somewhere unseen where it would likely die slowly from the wounds.

A hand brushed over Nora's and took hold of the spear. Nora released her grip and fumbled in the hazy darkness, her light beam illuminating nothing more than a thick mass of brown speckles in the water. Finding the spear AJ held in her other hand, Nora took the second weapon and quickly drew back against the band. Careful to avoid AJ, and working by feel, Nora sat the tips against the flailing fish and released the spear.

The fish jolted a few times before the resistance faded as it finally expired. They both slowly pulled the two spears away from the hull, and Nora could already taste the fish tacos this plump catch would give them. They raised up inside the engine room until the haze cleared, and they both shone their lights on their catch. Nora heard AJ talking into her regulator. It all came out as a groan underwater, but she had a pretty good idea of what her friend was saying.

Over the past few weeks, dive guides had been reporting an enormous lionfish inside the *Kittiwake* wreck. The invasive species had no natural predators in the Caribbean, unlike the South Pacific waters where they originated. For over twenty years, the lionfish population had spread prolifically and was wiping out smaller fish across the reefs. Attempts to persuade the local predators to attack the live fish had failed, so culling had become the only efficient means of controlling the problem.

Nora held her spear steady while AJ withdrew hers, tucking it into her waistband. She then shone her light at the exit, indicating it was time to go, and Nora waited until her friend eased away, then fell in line behind her. Before Nora made a single fin stroke, a huge green moray eel appeared in her light beam with its jaws open wide, revealing rows of terrifyingly sharp teeth. Nora had no time to move before the eel clamped its mouth around the lionfish and wrenched it from the spear tips, retreating into the darkness with the same speed it had attacked.

"*Fy faen!*" Nora groaned into her regulator.

AJ turned, sensing a commotion, and Nora held up her empty spear. AJ made a series of grunts into her regulator, which Nora assumed were expletives. She shrugged her shoulders. The stupid eels wouldn't take a live lionfish, but they'd scavenge a diver's kill despite the spines still being venomous after death. So much for tacos. Nora frowned and waved AJ toward the exit with her empty spear.

For the next five minutes, the two divers wound their way out of the shipwreck and kicked toward the coral bommie where AJ's Newton dive boat, *Hazel's Odyssey*, was moored to a Department of Environment buoy. At fifteen feet below the surface, they began their safety stop, where they would pause to allow their bodies' physiology to equalize before returning to atmospheric pressure.

Nora hung in the water column and switched off her flashlight. AJ did the same, and slowly their eyes adjusted to the darkness. A small blinking red light hung from the stern of AJ's boat; a safety beacon in case they became disoriented. Farther away, light glowed on the surface around the hull of a large yacht they'd seen moored to a larger buoy when they'd arrived. The extravagant boat had been loaded with well-dressed guests enjoying an evening on the water.

Their three-minute safety stop ticked by, and the two women glided toward the ladder hanging down into the water from the stern of *Hazel's Odyssey*. Climbing the steps in the calm Caribbean waters a quarter of a mile from the famed Seven Mile Beach, they dropped their tanks and BCDs into the racks lining either side of the aft deck.

"Why did you leave him down there?" AJ asked in her soft English accent, grinning at her young Norwegian friend. "He would have fed us both!"

"I didn't let him go," Nora replied dryly with her Nordic accent. "Someone took him."

"Oh bugger! I missed that," AJ responded. "I didn't see any grouper or dog snappers in there."

Nora grabbed two Mermaid Divers beach towels from the covered cabin and tossed one to AJ. "Green moray."

"Bloody hell! A big one?"

"One bite, and he took him off the spear."

AJ cringed. "That's a big one."

"*Ja*. He followed me under the pipes, but I forgot about him," Nora explained, "until he came back for dinner."

They both slipped out of their 3mm wetsuits and began drying themselves after a quick freshwater rinse from a shower head plumbed into the rear frame of the flybridge support. Smooth jazz music and laughter echoed across the water from the luxury yacht as the two women put on hooded sweatshirts despite the balmy island night.

"Think they'd notice if we snuck aboard?" AJ said with a chuckle. "I bet they have some good nosh."

Nora stared at the sleek gray-and-white vessel with dark-tinted windows wrapping around both decks. Atop the upper deck, an open-sided flybridge sported an impressive array of navigation gear on its roof. The boat was well equipped for open ocean travel. People mingled and chatted on both levels of the long aft decks as waiters moved among them with trays of drinks and hors d'oeuvres.

"Gyro stabilizer," AJ said, pointing to the boat. "See how it doesn't rock at all?"

Nora nodded as their own much smaller thirty-six-foot boat rolled gently from side to side in the subtle swells.

"Let's dive again, or go," the Norwegian said, standing up.

AJ was used to her friend's abrupt nature, but she was still taken aback by the urgency to leave. She was about to protest before realizing she was being an idiot. Nora had been caught up in a human trafficking scheme a few years back where the underaged girls were made to escort older men. The lavish boat and the wealthy guests aboard were likely a painful reminder.

"We got what we came for," AJ said brightly. "Well, we had what we came for until you fed the biggest lionfish of all time to Mr. Eel."

Nora rolled her eyes. "I'll get the line," she replied flatly, and edged along the side of the cabin toward the bow.

AJ made her way up the aluminum ladder to the flybridge

and started the twin diesels, letting them idle and warm back up.

"They won't believe us, you know," she called down.

Nora shrugged her shoulders. "So?"

AJ frowned. "So... I want to be heralded as the lionfish queen."

"You're not," Nora retorted, stifling a grin.

"I meant *we* should be heralded with the honors."

"How many shots did you fire?" Nora asked.

"I bloody well helped, Viking; you needed my help!" AJ complained.

Nora shrugged her shoulders again. "You were *there* when I killed it."

AJ dropped *Hazel's Odyssey* into gear and edged forward, taking the slack from the line. "Stop talking nonsense and get the bloody line, will you?"

Nora released them from the buoy and stowed the rope, smirking the whole time. When she joined AJ at the helm, they were already idling past the mega yacht, which she noticed was named *DSTP*.

"What does that mean?" Nora asked, staring at the bold letters across the stern.

"Don't Spend The Principal," AJ replied. She didn't offer up the fact that she only knew because she'd asked the dockmaster in George Town harbor when she'd seen the boat tied up the day before.

"Huh," Nora grunted, and turned to look where they were going. "*Dritt!* Look out!"

"Oh bugger!" AJ yelped, seeing a small rigid inflatable boat, known as a RIB, crossing their path. She swung the wheel to port and bumped the right motor, veering sharply as the little tender skipped across the water off their starboard bow.

"Wanker!" AJ yelled. "Run some bloody lights!"

A man dressed in dark clothing stood at the small center console helm and never looked up, but a second figure in the bow glared at the two divers on *Hazel's Odyssey*. He also kept an arm around a woman perched next to him on the narrow seat. She was a beautiful strawberry blonde wearing an expensive-looking black, sequined dress. Her head bobbed with every wave as though she was taking a nap.

AJ straightened out the Newton, and they both watched the black-and-gray tender make for the shoreline farther south.

"What was that all about?" AJ grumbled.

Nora shook her head. "I don't know, but something wasn't right."

"You can say that again. Why were those berks mad at us?" AJ continued. "They're the ones running dark."

Nora thought for a moment. "The men were angry, but the woman…"

AJ scoffed. "She was plastered. Couldn't even hold her bloody head up."

Nora stared into the darkness where the RIB was barely visible by its silhouette against the lights from shore. "Maybe."

2

An hour earlier…

The Cabot Foundation's most significant donors had been invited to a dinner at the Ritz-Carlton on Grand Cayman. The invitation included a night cruise of the local waters, and several dozen guests had turned up on the dock, eyeing the luxury yacht that awaited them. All were impressed with its grandeur.

The guests were directed to the steps that ran up the side of the yacht to the middle level, where it opened into a salon with couches and chairs, sliding doors opening onto the stern, and what was normally the dining room had been turned into a bar area with seating.

Harper sidled up to Rella, her green eyes twinkling with amusement. "How do you plan to weasel cash out of these richie folks when I haven't heard you once ask if they have their checkbooks on them?"

Rella Cabot, a striking blonde, was always impeccably dressed, and tonight was no different; in her slinky silver crystal beaded evening gown, she outshone the rest of the women. Unlike most of them, she didn't judge or look down her nose at anyone.

"Harper Finn, behave." Rella smirked, *at least try* on her face. "I can't thank you enough for agreeing to come on this fundraising cruise with me. Pryce was adamant that I not come by myself. He didn't want to hear that the chances of anything going wrong were close to nil. If he knew that we were out exploring the island yesterday…" Her brows went up. "But we did have a great time."

"Husbands! I had to listen to a lecture from Grey about not looking for trouble. As if…" Harper said, managing to paste on an innocent expression, and Rella laughed.

"The speech you gave to your guests was great," Harper continued, "and listing all the things your foundation does for people was not only impressive but inspiring. You're amazing."

"Most of the guests are regular donors who'd only need to make a phone call to increase their donation." Rella surveyed the room. "There are a couple of new faces, and I need to introduce myself. It's my hope that a cruise on this amazing yacht will loosen their pockets."

Rella's parents had started the Cabot Foundation. When they died in a private plane crash, Rella stepped in as CEO, pouring her energy into helping women's and children's charities. She never hesitated to use her connections to help people and recently began supporting animal rescues. When she took over, she'd vowed to make sure the foundation would continue to be a success, and thus far, she'd more than succeeded.

"It's clear that you're the star of the evening. A couple of the men can't keep their creepy eyes off you." Harper nudged Rella, letting her know which direction to look. It didn't surprise her that one of the men continued to stare, an inviting grin on his face, but the other disappeared in a blink. She looked around and couldn't catch sight of him anywhere.

"Everyone that received an invitation is a well-respected businessman or woman, many from the Miami area," Rella assured her. "It looks good for their companies to say that they support charities."

"Incoming." Harper tapped her elbow.

Two tuxedo-clad men who'd had their eyes on them all night and were old enough to be their fathers approached, confident they'd get lucky despite wearing wedding bands.

"Be nice," Rella said with raised brows and then flashed her CEO smile.

When the men asked them to dance, Rella winked at Harper over her partner's shoulder as she allowed herself to be led away.

"Hey, hon." The man next to Harper leered at her like she was a tasty morsel. "Ant... Antony." He extended his stubby hand.

The stutter in the immaculately dressed man's introduction led Harper to believe he'd given her a false name.

"Sally," she mumbled. Two could play at that game. She deliberately spoke quietly enough that he couldn't hear her, noting that it didn't bother him enough to ask her to repeat herself. He tugged her over to the small space in front of the bar where several couples were dancing.

"You're new to this crowd." The man leered, pulling her tighter against him as he swung her around and slid his hand down to her butt.

Harper was about to step all over his toes to bring the dance to an end when an ample-sized woman cut in and pushed her out of the way with a growl. Harper responded with a big grin. Eager to be free of the man, she didn't hesitate to slip away, sliding out the side doors that opened onto a walkway and leaned on the railing to enjoy the lights that flickered off the water.

She'd barely had a chance to enjoy the evening air when a swarthy man in a dark suit approached, tray in hand, and offered her champagne. He handed her one of the two glasses and took the other for himself, ditching the tray overboard.

"That's hardly environmentally friendly. Let's hope you didn't clock some unsuspecting fish," Harper said. *Dickface*.

"I've had my eye on you all night and couldn't resist the opportunity to meet you." He clinked his glass against hers.

He didn't bother with an introduction, and she didn't either.

"What's a beautiful woman doing out here all by herself?"

His penetrating stare had Harper looking over her shoulder to ensure the door was still open. If a scream became necessary, she knew it would only garner a few stares, but a kick to the groin would allow her to dash inside right into the middle of the dancing couples. "Waiting for my husband."

"If you were mine, I wouldn't leave you to the wolves on this boat."

"Does that include you?"

He laughed. "I'm here to support the foundation and all the good works it does." It sounded rehearsed.

Harper grabbed the railing, suddenly overcome with dizziness, and shook her head, strawberry-blond hair flying across her vision, making her head whirl even harder. She knew she'd eaten, so why? It definitely wasn't the two glasses of champagne. Time to get inside and make her way to one of the couches. "It was nice meeting you." She turned and stumbled.

The man caught her, jerking her to his side and tightening his hold. "Here, let me help you." He turned her away from the open doors, and she attempted to struggle. Unfortunately, all her efforts only resulted in him tightening his grip. "You need fresh air, and there's seating down this way." He led her toward the bow of the boat.

Harper barely had the energy to put one foot in front of the other and suddenly realized she must have been drugged. It was her last thought as everything went black.

3

Nora moved to the bow as AJ guided the Newton toward a dive buoy a hundred yards from shore. With practiced ease, the two women tied into the mooring, shut everything down, and secured the boat for the night. Nora used a boat hook to snag a second line on the mooring, untied it, and led two kayaks around the starboard side to the stern.

Hazel's Odyssey gently rocked as the almost nonexistent swells rolled toward the ironshore-lined coast just north of Seven Mile Beach. They dropped into the kayaks and paddled toward a bright streetlight in the parking lot for the public dock. AJ shared the smaller dock next door with her friend and mentor, Reg Moore. He operated three Newton dive boats, but for safety they moored all their boats offshore overnight.

Nora kept looking south although all she could see was lights from the hotels and condos, and a glow from the yacht tied to the *Kittiwake* wreck.

"Probably got pissed and made an arse of herself, so they took her ashore," AJ said, picking up on her friend's concern.

Nora's kayak bumped against the wooden dock, and she deftly scrambled up the framework, holding the tether in her hand. AJ followed suit and they hauled the kayaks onto the deck, then carried them up the jetty to a small hut signed Pearl Divers. A second sign depicting a mermaid, diver's helmet, and an anchor, had the words Mermaid Divers over the top.

"I'm starving," AJ said, as they used a chain to secure the little boats to the side of the building. "Fox and Hare?"

Nora was hungry too, and short of driving aimlessly around in the dark checking every spot a RIB could pull up, there was nothing she could do to ease her curiosity. "Okay."

They climbed in Nora's faded blue 1987 CJ-7 Jeep, and the young Norwegian let the engine warm up for a few minutes.

"I don't think she was passed out drunk," she said, struggling to take her mind off what she'd seen.

"What makes you say that?" AJ asked dubiously.

"She wouldn't stay passed out from booze in a bouncing boat like that."

"Maybe she was really, really shit-faced," AJ countered.

Nora shook her head. "Have you ever passed out drunk?"

"No, but I've had a few, and slept through all kinds of goings on. Have you?" AJ added, figuring she knew the answer.

"No. But several times a week we arrest someone for D and D. I've never had one who was completely comatose. They moan and groan and fuss and throw up."

"Well, perhaps you just saw your first."

Nora wasn't convinced, but she backed out of the spot, and pulled to the road, ready to turn left toward the pub.

AJ's cell phone rang. "Hang on a mo," she said, holding up a hand before answering the call. "Hey, Reg."

Between the road noise from the off-road tires and wind across the topless jeep, phone calls were impossible while in motion. AJ bantered back and forth for a minute while Reg gave her a hard time for not bringing the lionfish home for supper. AJ finally hung up.

"Turn right," she instructed Nora. "We're going to Reg and Pearl's. He said she's made enough fish and chips to feed an army."

Nora spun the wheel to the right and three minutes later, after winding around the little streets of West Bay, she parked in the driveway of a single-level home with a well-maintained front yard. Reg stood in the doorway, his large frame filling most of the space, but his dog, Coop, slipped past his legs and raced over to the two women. They squatted down and Coop offered them his belly for scratches while his tail never stopped wagging.

"Food's getting cold," Reg growled in his deep voice with a London accent. "Coop. Here."

The Cayman brown hound, as the mixed breed prolific on the island was known, leapt up and bounded over to the big man's feet, wagging his tail even more. Coop's enthusiasm rather shattered Reg's tough guy facade, and he grinned at the mutt.

"Get inside, you silly bloody sod," he muttered.

Everything about the home was simple, tasteful, and tidy. Pearl was responsible for all of it, as Reg would have Land Rover parts scattered across the kitchen table if left to his own devices. Reg's wife was a short but full-figured woman, in her fifties, but no one would ever guess. She had wavy blond hair and a beautiful smile. She hugged AJ and Nora in turn.

"Sit down, sit down," she said, pointing to the dining table beside the open-plan kitchen.

Two large plates were already set out, piled high with breaded fish on one and fries on the other. Two serving bowls had steam rising from baked beans and peas.

"Blimey, Pearl, you were expecting an army," AJ said, pulling up a chair.

Pearl set a bottle of white wine on the table and rolled her eyes. "Somebody was supposed to invite you two earlier today." Her eyes turned on Reg, who scratched his bushy gray beard and pretended not to hear her.

"In his defense, Pearl," AJ began with a straight face, "I only saw Reg ten or fifteen times today, so he didn't have much chance to say anything…"

"This looks splendid, love," Reg interrupted, snagging a piece of fish with a pair of tongs. "Of course, would have been nice to have that fresh lionfish we were promised."

"Oh, listen to his nibs over here," AJ retorted. "I offered for you to come along, but you declined. Maybe you could have been a gentleman and wrestled the moray while Nora brought our prize home."

Nora and Pearl both grinned as the two barbed back and forth a while longer. They finally quit ribbing each other so they could eat. Pearl poured wine for the three of them. Reg already had a Seven Fathoms rum over ice which he raised in the air.

"Cheers then," he said. "And thanks for putting all this together, love," he continued, winking at his wife.

The others raised their wine glasses, and the two guests added their thanks.

AJ looked down to where Coop had his chin resting on her leg, reminding her he was starving to death. At least his eyes conveyed that message.

"Don't you dare," Reg grunted, waggling his knife in AJ's direction.

"I wouldn't dream of it," AJ replied, feigning shock at the suggestion.

"Right. That's why he comes straight to you every time," Reg said, shaking his head. "You're the soft touch."

"He just loves me best," AJ said proudly, biding her time to slip Coop a French fry or two.

"How was the dive, then?" Pearl asked, in between bites.

"It was fun," AJ replied. "And we got what we went for. I'm telling you; it was the biggest lionfish I've ever seen."

"The ones nobody else sees are always the record breakers, eh?" Reg jibed.

"Nora saw it too!" AJ replied. "Tell him, Nora."

The Norwegian slowly sipped her wine and took her time responding. "*Nora's* the one who shot him," she said, and carried on eating.

Reg roared with laughter, pointing to AJ. "Did that one even help?"

Nora nodded. "She handed me a second spear to finish him off."

"See!" AJ yelped. "I was in the thick of it, too."

Nora loved to hear her friends messing with each other, but she still couldn't shake the vision of the lady in the black dress from her mind.

"There was a yacht moored on the big buoy," she said, looking at Reg. "It's called the *DSTP*. Know anything about it?"

Reg finished chewing. "I've seen it in the harbor. Brought down from Miami is what I heard. Some yacht broker geezer."

"They were having quite the shindig," AJ said. "Fancy event of some sort. All dressed up. Some plonkers in a tender were running around with no lights on. We almost ran them over."

"Who would know about the boat?" Nora asked.

"Thinking of buying it?" Reg replied with a chuckle.

Nora ignored his joke. "I want to know who owns it and what the party was about."

Reg frowned. "Did something happen?"

AJ shook her head. "Just the tender thing. But there was a woman in the RIB with two blokes, and it did look a bit suspicious. The Viking bloodhound here thinks she's on a scent."

Pearl looked at her husband. "You have a mate with customs, don't you?"

Reg nodded. "I do, but I'd be putting him in a bind asking. He's not supposed to disclose any details."

"What about Ben?" AJ asked. "He might know."

"Worth a try," Reg replied, but before either he or AJ could dig up the number for their friend with the Royal Cayman Islands Police Service Joint Marine Unit, Nora had her cell phone ringing on speaker phone.

"Blimey. You only have six numbers in there," AJ laughed and fluttered her eyelashes. "And one of them is Ben, huh?"

Nora ignored her, and a Caymanian-accented voice answered the call. "Dis is Ben."

"Hey. It's Nora. I had a question for you," she said with her usual lack of polite preamble. "You know anything about the big yacht, *DSTP*?"

"Nora," he said, his voice brightening. "How you bin, young lady?"

"Fine," she replied with a frown creasing her forehead. "Do you know the boat?"

He laughed, his deep voice reflecting his size, which was taller than Reg and just as broad in the chest and shoulders.

"Hi Ben, you're on speaker. This is AJ, and Reg is with us."

Nora now frowned at her friend for wasting time.

"Hello, Miss AJ. You got da big fella dere too. Dis must be real important," he said, laughing again.

"Well?" Nora intervened before more chitchat could take place.

"I know it. Took da customs guys aboard when it arrived."

"Why is it here?"

"Dey havin' a charity fundraiser event on da boat. Den headin' back to Miami, best I know."

"We saw it tied up to the big mooring on the *Kittiwake* tonight," AJ explained. "Looked like they were having a posh do."

"Dere you go den," Ben replied. "Somet'ing happen, or you just curious?"

AJ looked at Nora, who shrugged her shoulders. Nora knew her friend would end up talking anyway, so she let her begin.

"We just about ran over a RIB tender leaving the yacht in the dark without any running lights," AJ told him. "Two blokes and a woman on board. She looked a bit worse for wear."

"How do you mean?" Ben asked in a more serious tone.

"She looked like she'd passed out drunk, if you ask me, but Nora thinks it might be something else."

The line was silent for a few moments. "Like what, Nora?" he asked.

"I'm not sure," she admitted. "I just had a bad feeling about it."

"I see. Should I be sendin' a patrol boat out dere?"

"No," Nora said firmly. "The tender was making for shore. Whatever went on had already happened. And maybe it was nothing."

"Okay. I'll keep an eye out tomorrow," Ben promised.

"Who owns the yacht?" Nora asked.

"Paperwork had da boat registered to da company, Magic

City Luxury Yacht Sales and Charter. Da captain said he a contract guy. Works for dem when dey need him."

"No one from the company aboard?" Reg asked.

"No, sir. I heard da captain telling customs da boss flyin' in and meetin' dem here. Dat was two days ago, so guess da man here if dey had da event already."

"What's his name?" Nora asked.

"Da captain?"

"The owner," Nora clarified impatiently.

"Dat I don't know, but da customs guy, Jaden, he got his business card from da captain, I believe. I can text him and ask."

"What are you doing tomorrow morning?" Nora asked.

"Usual. Office by eight, den we'll go on patrol, or whatever comes up."

"Meet me at the harbor at seven, and get the name." Nora felt the stares from everyone at the table. "*Takk*," she added.

"I was goin' to…"

They didn't hear any more from Ben, as Nora ended the call.

"Isn't he about ten ranks above you?" AJ asked.

"*Ja*," Nora said, and took a sip of her wine.

AJ chuckled and shook her head.

4

Where the heck was Harper? Rella groaned inwardly as she looked around at her guests for the umpteenth time—some still drinking and dancing. But she still hadn't seen her friend again anywhere. Thus far, the night had gone well; donations were up, and all appeared to be having a good time. She'd made her way around the main salon of the yacht and danced or talked with every guest until her feet hurt. She was ready to kick off the crystal-laden stilettos that matched her dress. She eyed them and wondered, not for the first time, why they couldn't make a stylish shoe that was also comfortable.

Blake Decker approached, cutting into her thoughts, and she stepped forward with a big smile. It was his company that had made this fine yacht available and had also made several recommendations for staffing. "I want to thank you for all you did to make this party such a big success."

"Ms. Cabot." His smile was wide. "It's been a pleasure. I wish all our clients were as easy to please." An employee called to Decker and motioned him over. "I'll catch up with you later. Know that if you need anything at all, all you have to do is ask."

Where was Harper? The question rankled, but she easily kept her smile in place as she worked the room. Thinking back… Rella had last seen her when they'd both been asked to dance by men who hoped to conclude the evening horizontal in one of the staterooms.

The strings of lights that could be seen on one side of the yacht confirmed that they'd docked. Rella laughed, envisioning giving her guests a slight push to get them to disembark in a speedy fashion. A few were already lined up and ready to call it a night. Now for the rest of them.

She beelined for the bar and grabbed the attention of Bolger, the bartender, who'd been a favorite with the women all night—surfer body, boy-next-door looks, and an easy-going smile. It hadn't bothered any of the men when the women flirted with him and he with them. "If anyone wants another drink, tell them the lobby bar inside the Ritz will do refills at no charge—all they have to do is show their ticket. If they don't want to hear that this bar is closed, tell them you have nine kids you need to get home to."

Bolger scrunched up his nose and shook his head. "That just might get me bigger tips."

Another couple rushed up to say goodnight. "As always, we had a great time," they gushed.

Rella walked the couple out to the walkway, where several more guests were lined up and ready to make their way down the steps. With a pasted-on smile, she thanked them and shook hands. Only a handful of stragglers remained, and though they appeared reluctant, they slowly made their way to the exit. There was still no sign of Harper. Whatever she was up to, the woman had proven she could take care of herself, so Rella wouldn't worry just yet.

Bolger flagged her back to the bar. "Do you need anything before I cut out of here?"

"No, thank you. You did a great job, and the guests loved you."

"Several wanted to know where they could go and continue their fun until the early hours, and I was happy to offer a few suggestions."

Rella took another scan of the room. "Have you, by chance, seen my friend—strawberry blonde, same height as me, black sequined dress?"

"I remember her; we talked earlier in the evening. After that, I saw her making the rounds, talking to the guests; she looked to be having fun." Bolger also scanned the room and craned his neck to look outside. "Though I haven't seen her in a while. Maybe she needed a moment to herself in one of the staterooms?"

"You're probably right. Well, goodnight. Have fun with all those kids of yours."

He laughed.

All the guests had now made their way off the yacht, except for one man on his phone in the corner. He didn't appear to need anything, so she turned to one of the passageways that led to the staterooms. She opened the door to the room assigned to them in case they needed to freshen up, crossed the floor, pushed a painting aside, and opened the safe. Harper's purse still sat alongside hers.

"There's no way she'd leave this boat without saying a word to me," Rella said to herself as she reclosed the safe and made her way back to the salon.

The lone guest now sat on the arm of one of the couches, a penetrating stare and slimy smile on his face. She slipped her practiced smile back into place and approached the man. "I want to thank you for coming." She hoped he'd get the hint, as the only people left on the boat now were employees.

"You looking for your friend?" His dark eyes, pupils almost pinpricks, appeared to strip her clothes off.

Rella stiffened, bristling at the idea that he would try to intimidate her. "Have you seen her?"

"Briefly. She was leaving the yacht with her date."

Rella didn't have the patience for whatever he was up to. They hadn't been docked that long, and she would've seen Harper disembark. The very least Harper would have done was tell her she was leaving. And she highly doubted that her friend would go off with another man, being happily married. But if by chance he was right, something was wrong, and Rella needed to go after her. "If you'll excuse me."

The man blocked her. "Your friend—Harper, isn't it? I thought you'd want to know that she's comfortable… for now. But if you want her back in one piece, it'll cost you."

His words registered, but what he was suggesting… Fear danced up her spine. His eyes bored into her, daring her to punch the smugness off his face. Harper always had her phone on her and always answered it. Knowing that, Rella pulled out her phone.

The man slid in front of her and sent the phone sailing through the open door. "Let's get something straight—you will not ignore me. You think your money makes you better than everyone else, but you're about to discover that you're wrong. What it does is put you in a special category."

He stood so close, Rella could feel him breathing and took a step back. He moved with her until she was pressed against the wall.

She forced icy calm into her veins and said, "Pretty sure we haven't been introduced."

"My name isn't important. What is important is that you've got one chance to get your friend back. If her life means nothing to you, the fish in the channel could use a good meal once she's no longer useful to us." He bared his teeth in a creepy smile.

"You're telling me that you have my friend and are holding her for—"

"Ransom?" His beady brown eyes never left her face. "It's not necessary to use such an unfriendly word. How about we say payment for keeping her comfortable and safe?"

If she could get hold of Harper's husband, she had no doubt it would be this man who'd become fish food, but she knew the man in front of her would make sure she never made that phone call. She racked her brain for some way to ensure nothing terrible happened to Harper. "I'll need proof of life."

"To show you what a nice guy I am…" He pulled out his phone. "I'm certain that Harper's current digs aren't what she's used to, but if she does what she's told—and more importantly, if you do—things could improve." He flicked across the screen and turned it around to show a video of Harper sitting on a dirty floor, looking cautiously around, her back to the wall and her hands zip-tied in front of her.

He played it twice. Rella's husband would have told her to call the police, but that wasn't an option with her phone who knew where, and she doubted this man would let her out of his sight long enough to contact anyone, expecting her to try to do just that. Also, she didn't know how law enforcement in a foreign country would handle it and whether it might hasten Harper's death.

Desperately trying to think what Harper's husband, Grey, would do, and seeing he wasn't about to give her any time to think, she hit on, "It's clear that Harper was alive when the video was shot, but what assurance do I have that she's alive now?"

The man shook his head. "You're not very good at this, are

you? You'll see your little buddy shortly, or you can yell and scream, in which case she'll be dead within the minute."

Rella's dread increased. "How much?"

"I'm not the one who'll determine the amount. But from what I've heard about you, what's a billion or two?"

"If not you, then who?" Rella bit out, trying hard to control herself and losing the battle.

"Calm down. If you and your friend want to walk away, you'll do what you're told." He trailed his finger down the V of her dress.

Rella smacked it back out, barely refraining from trying to snap it in half. "You want your money? Keep your hands to yourself."

"Your life is in my hands." He pulled a gun from his waistband behind his back and pushed it against her chest. "Go ahead, scream; see where that gets you. Sure, one of the staff will come running... and they'll just end up dead next to you. And know that I'll take out a few more on my way to the ride that awaits me."

"I'll cooperate." In a bold move, Rella pushed the muzzle of the gun to one side, doubting that he'd pull the trigger when he wanted her money.

"We're going to walk out of here like we're a couple in love and climb into the boat waiting at the dock. Then you'll join your friend."

"Why not stay here and make the transfer? Once it's completed, you can release Harper and tell me where to pick her up."

"I call the shots, not you, Ms. CEO, so get over thinking you're in charge. We both know that getting the kind of cash we're talking about isn't as simple as writing a check." He rolled his eyes. "You'll be supervised while you transfer the funds."

He was beyond stupid if he thought that kind of money could be transferred with a few clicks on a keyboard either. She only hoped whoever else was involved didn't know that there were security alerts she could activate to track the money without their knowledge.

"Are you ready?" He held out his arm, clearly expecting her to take it.

Rella stared, knowing that leaving with him was a bad idea. But the other option was dying here and leaving Harper to meet the same fate. She reluctantly took his arm.

As they walked, she mulled over her options but couldn't come up with a way to get Harper and herself out of this situation. Nor was she confident that transferring a large sum of money would ensure they'd walk away in one piece. He led her through the salon door at the rear, out to the upper deck and the stairs leading down to the stern. With each step, she took in her surroundings with an eagle eye. She looked down into the darkened water, thought about diving in, and dismissed the idea—if it were just her life on the line, then maybe, but not while they had Harper.

"You're certainly being a gentleman," she told the man as he gripped her arm and guided her down the stairs.

"You think so?" He chuckled. "It's all about your bank balance, hon." On the broad swim step at the stern, he pointed to her stilettos. "You might want to take those off before you fall; can't have you breaking your leg." His tone made it clear he couldn't care less if that happened.

Bending down, Rella took her pricey shoes off and hooked the straps over her index finger.

Nestled against the stern was a black-and-gray tender with another man at the wheel. She stepped on board and took a seat. Her chaperone clapped the driver on the shoulder—a hulk of a man—and seconds later, the boat shot across the water. Rella managed to swallow her yelp. She thought about her husband and promised herself that she'd do whatever she had to do to ensure she got back home to him and her life in Miami. She was an astute businesswoman who knew how to make a deal and would use the skills she'd honed to negotiate her and Harper's release. When her abductor pulled out his phone, Rella told him, "If that's your boss, make sure he understands that he doesn't get one cent if Harper's hurt in any way."

"You need a reminder that you're not calling the shots. Surprised you're not smart enough to have figured that out already," he said, his fingers clicking across the screen. He selected a picture and held it out, showing Harper with her back to the camera, curled up in a fetal position in the corner of a small room.

"How about I make a deal with you?" Rella asked. "You can cut the others out that way—more money for you." Before his face went blank, she saw that he liked the idea.

"Now it's *you* thinking that *I'm* the stupid one," he barked out a laugh. "That little plan of yours is a good way to get me killed."

Turning away, Rella found it hard to see anything. The boat's lights didn't illuminate much on the dark water. The ride was short, and the driver soon cruised up alongside another dock. This time, Mr. Personality left Rella to climb out on her own, which was challenging in her tight dress. The entire time, he stood back and smirked. As soon as she was on the dock, the boat took off.

Bare feet and a wood-splintered dock made for a painful walk, despite stepping gingerly. "Since I won't be needing these…" She held up her heels and made a show of throwing them into the water. Hopefully, he wouldn't notice that she'd only pitched one shoe and left the other on the dock. She hoped it would somehow be linked to her when it was found. She wasn't sure how, but it was worth a try.

A black SUV waited in the sloped parking lot, and she was shoved toward it.

"Hurry up," he grumped, holding open the back door. Once she was in, he slammed the door and got behind the wheel. Rella tried the door handle, but the child safety locks were engaged. She rolled her eyes—like she was going to bail out of the back of the SUV when he had Harper. He revved the engine and pulled up to a two-lane road she thought might be the frontage street into downtown. He turned left, then used several short streets in quick succession before finally turning sharply into a field of some sort. It was dark with a few pinpricks of lights from buildings far to the left, and a handful of security lights on tall poles illuminated single-story warehouse buildings beyond a tall fence to her right.

He'd taken out his phone and was now arguing with someone, but he kept his voice down, except for the occasional slip, and Rella couldn't make out a word. The SUV bumped along a dirt trail until her kidnapper parked in front of a yellow shipping container. In the headlight beams she noticed a door and a window. An office maybe? It was hard to make out what it was used for.

He got out, opened the back, and dragged Rella across the seat. She stumbled, and he reached out at the last second to keep her from falling on the uneven ground. He jerked her to her feet and led her over to the shipping container.

"Don't you think it's time we introduced ourselves?" Rella asked.

He snorted.

"Okay, then how about if I just call you Moron?" *That's exactly what you are*, she left unsaid. Not surprisingly, he didn't like her name for him. She'd known that would be the case and knew she should've bit it back when he squeezed her forearm so hard, she could feel bruises forming.

"It's Zeus." He unlocked the door, which was in the middle of the building with a steel-barred window next to it. When she failed to step inside the darkened space, he shoved her hard enough that she tripped and barely kept herself from falling on her face. He flipped on a dim light, gripped her arm, marched her to the opposite end of the large dark space, and stopped in front of the only other door. He opened it and shoved her inside. "Be a good guest until I come back to get you."

Before the door slammed and the room was plunged into darkness, Rella made out the form of Harper in the corner just as she heard the lock turn with an ominous scrape. A faint light came from under the door, but it was hard to see farther than her nose. She scrambled over to her friend and sank down next to her. "You better be okay," she whispered in her ear.

Harper turned toward her friend. "I was pretending to be out of it to see if he—whoever he is—would come closer."

"When he refused to give me his name, I tried to nickname him Moron, and that motivated him to tell me it's actually Zeus. Which is nearly as bad as Moron."

"I know you can't see me, even with that trace of light coming from under the door, but I'm rolling my eyes. I was out of it, but I remember hearing them refer to each other as Zeus and Apollo. Anyway… I planned that when he came over to check on me—if he did—I'd poke both his eyes out, hoping he'd drop his gun. Then I'd pick up his gun and shoot him."

"What were you going to use to do the eye poking?" Rella pulled Harper into a hard hug, then turned, so they had their backs to the wall.

"Jam my fingers right in his eyeballs. Brings a person to

their knees," Harper said with assurance and held up her hands, making jabbing motions. "So happy to see you, but also annoyed, as I wanted you to be out there raising hell."

"Your planned fight scene is so…" Rella cringed, refusing to commit that mental picture to memory.

"Effective is the word you're looking for."

5

Ben strode down the dock in his Royal Cayman Islands Police Service Joint Marine Unit uniform. His large frame filled what she guessed was the largest size available from the police store. Nora wore her constable's uniform, ready for her shift starting at 8:00 a.m. back in West Bay. At five-foot-nine, she still felt dwarfed by the good-looking dark-skinned man. She handed him a cup of coffee in a compostable paper cup and lid.

"Good morning," he responded, taking the coffee. "T'anks."

"Hey," she greeted him, and sipped from her own travel mug.

They both turned to look at the Azimut Grande 36M moored at the concrete pier used for overflow cruise ship tenders in the small Hog Sty Bay harbor. The only other vessels in the U-shaped bay were the dive boats lined up along a neighboring jetty, their crews busy preparing for the day.

"What are you hopin' to achieve here, Nora?" Ben asked.

It was a good question, and one Nora had pondered at length before she fell asleep last night, and since she'd woken at 5:15 a.m. that morning. She still didn't have a good answer, just a nagging knot in her stomach which told her something wasn't right.

"We'll poke a stick and see what comes running out," she replied and walked toward the luxury yacht.

"Nora…" Ben called after her, taking a couple of long strides to catch up. "We can't go disturbin' dese folks for no reason, now."

"We have a reason," she replied flatly, without breaking stride.

"*You* have a curiosity," he pointed out. "*We* don't have an official reason."

"Did you find out who owns the boat?" Nora asked, ignoring Ben's concern.

"Dat company outa Miami I told you about. Magic City Luxury Yacht Sales and Charter."

Nora stopped, and Ben about ran into her. "But you said you'd ask about the actual owner."

Ben shook his head and groaned. "I did. Some guy named Decker. I t'ink he owns da charter business."

"Hmm," Nora grunted, and continued in the shadow of the sleek hull of the 115-foot-long dark-tinted windowed yacht.

A crew member in navy blue shorts and a white polo shirt with a logo and the name "DSTP" embroidered on the left chest, watched them approach. The name "Kevin" was embroidered on the right side. He stood on the large stern swim step and smiled.

"Good morning," the young man said in an Australian accent, his smile broadening as he looked Nora over. "How can I help you?"

"Does your yacht have a tender?" Nora asked without introduction.

"I wish it was my yacht, love," Kevin said with a laugh. "But yeah, course it does."

Nora looked from stern to bow and couldn't see a davit. "Where is it?"

The Australian laughed again. "In the garage," he said, pointing to the starboard side against the dock. "Why? What's got you coppers up this early to ask about our tender?"

Nora considered her reply and decided she wasn't ready to divulge too much yet. "Can we see it?"

Kevin's brow furrowed, and his smile evaporated. "I'd better get the captain before I let you lot on, love. This sounds like something above my pay grade. The captain likes to handle stuff like this."

"You're not paid enough to show us a dinghy?" Nora replied.

"We don't need to be disturbin' da captain and all dat," Ben cut in. "How about you describe da tender for us?"

Nora scowled at Ben.

"Perhaps I can help you?" came a voice from the main deck.

An impeccably groomed man in his fifties dressed in a sport blazer looked down upon them and smiled.

"Sorry to disturb you, sir," Kevin blurted. "They were asking about tenders and such."

"Yes," the man said, maintaining his smile, which displayed his perfect, white teeth. "I'm Blake Decker. I run the sales and charter business who owns this yacht. We'd be happy to help you in any way possible, Constable…?"

"Sommer," Nora replied. "And this is Officer Ben Crooks from the Joint Marine Unit."

"Nice to meet you both. Please come aboard." Decker replied. "Kevin, show them our tender below, and I'll be down in a few moments to answer any questions."

"Certainly, sir. This way," Kevin said, his smile slowly returning, although his hopeful and flirty looks toward Nora had vanished.

Ben let Nora go first across the short gangway from the dock to the swim step, and they followed Kevin past cushioned lounge chairs through a doorway in the stern. Ben had to duck, but not much. They entered a walkway where Kevin opened another door into the toy garage, revealing a WaveRunner sitting alongside a white-hulled RIB. The Australian stepped out of the way so Nora could look inside.

As with the appearance of the exterior, the inside of the yacht was polished to a shimmering finish and spotlessly clean. Even in the so-called garage Nora figured you could eat off the floor. Neither toy looked as though it had ever been used.

"This the only one?" Nora asked.

"Tender?" Kevin responded. "Yeah. We can squeeze four people on it if we had to, but it's really for two. The *DSTP* has been a display boat at dock in Miami, mostly. Chartered for parties, like last night's."

Nora stepped back and let Kevin close the watertight door to the garage. "Were you aboard last night?"

"Sure," he said, leading them back to the stern lounging area and swim step. "But once we tied up, we were off duty. Just hung out on the bridge until we took her back in."

"You didn't go to the party?" Ben asked.

Kevin scoffed. "They hired local caterers," he replied, then switched to a whisper. "And crew don't mingle with guests. If you know what I mean?"

"What else can we help you with?" Decker asked, descending the stairs from the main deck. "Would you like to come inside and have breakfast?" he added.

"No, thank you, sir," Ben quickly replied, shaking the man's offered hand. "I think we have all we needed."

Decker moved to Nora and shook her hand. "May I ask why the interest in tenders?"

"Did you see a black RIB come out to the boat last night?" Nora asked.

Decker thought for a moment. "To my knowledge, we took all our guests and staff from the dock here and returned them to the same place. We didn't have any boats running back and forth." He turned to Kevin. "Do you recall seeing anything?"

"There was a dive boat on the wreck," Kevin replied. "They arrived after us and left before us, but that was a thirty, maybe thirty-five-foot v-hull. Other than that, I don't remember anyone else."

"A black RIB with three people on board was seen leaving your yacht at the same time the divers headed in," Nora continued. "Is there anyone else who might have seen them?"

"I assume the divers are the witnesses to this black RIB," Decker said. "Could they have seen someone who was simply passing by? Curious perhaps, taking a look at the party?"

"That could well have been what was happenin', sir," Ben said, taking a step toward the gangway.

"I was on the dive boat," Nora said firmly. "A black RIB was leaving your yacht with two men and a woman aboard."

"I see," Decker said thoughtfully. "And you'd like to track down these people for some reason?"

"My reason is concern for the safety of the woman in the dinghy," Nora replied. "So yes, I'd like to track these people down."

Decker looked genuinely shocked, or surprised. Perhaps both, Nora wasn't sure.

"My God," he said, touching his hand to his forehead. "Kevin, ask the captain to meet us in the main salon, please."

Kevin trotted up the curved stairs, and Decker followed at a more controlled pace. "Please, come with me," he said, not waiting for a response. "I had no idea it was something this serious."

Ben politely let Nora go first, and they chased Decker up the steps to the main deck where an outdoor lounge area shaded by the upper deck led to the main salon. Decker took them inside past a lavish curved sofa to a large ten-person dining table.

Nora looked around before taking a seat at the table. She wondered how late the staff had worked to return the whole boat to the spotless condition it was now in. It was hard to imagine a party had taken place there.

"Coffee?" Becker asked, pouring himself a cup from a silver carafe.

Nora held up her stainless-steel travel mug. "No thanks."

Ben also declined, placing his paper cup on the table, so Decker sat.

"Can you give me a description of the woman you saw, Constable Sommer? I met most of the guests throughout the evening, perhaps I can help identify her."

"Black dress, blonde hair," Nora replied, knowing her details were thin.

Decker nodded. "I'm afraid that only rules out the male guests. As you can imagine, a soiree such as our event draws a large attendance of ladies in their finest black evening gowns. Did you see her face?"

Nora shook her head. "Not clearly."

Decker paused a moment before continuing. "Well, we had a photographer aboard, so he would have pictures of every guest," he said, taking his cell phone from his pocket. "I'll reach out and have him send you everything we have."

Ben held a hand up. "This all might be over nuttin' at all,

sir, so let's not inconvenience anyone or make too much fuss as yet."

Decker smiled. "It's no trouble at all, Officer. Better we get this sorted and make sure this woman is safe than delay and miss an opportunity to help someone in need." He tapped out a text and hit send. "Besides, the guests last night are friends, clients, and contributors. I have a personal interest in their well-being."

"What was the party for?" Nora asked, after kicking Ben under the table.

"A fundraiser for The Cabot Foundation," Decker replied.

"What's that?" Nora asked bluntly.

Decker smiled again. Nora wasn't certain whether it was a condescending "you ought to know that name" smile or an innocent pleasantry. His soft hazel eyes suggested the latter. "A friend of mine, Rella Cabot, runs the foundation raising money for various charities supporting women and children in need."

A man entered the salon wearing a white uniform shirt with four stripes and an anchor on each epaulet. His face was meticulously clean-shaven, and his dark eyes flitted from one person to the next. Nora guessed him to be in his early forties, then amended her estimation to late forties when he removed his uniform cap to reveal receding short brown hair.

"Ah, Captain Hall, thank you for joining us," Decker said, standing. "This is Constable Sommer and Officer Crooks from local law enforcement. They're investigating a tender that was seen near us last night. Near the wreck mooring."

"A tender?" the captain replied with a furrowed brow. "We didn't tender anyone to the *DSTP*, sir. In fact, our tender hasn't left the garage since we arrived."

"Yes, they've seen ours, captain, and it doesn't match the black RIB Miss Sommer saw last night."

"A black RIB?" the captain repeated. "I don't recall any tenders coming or going last night, sir. Black, white, or any other color."

Decker nodded. "Neither did I, but I thought it prudent to check with you. Thank you, Captain."

"So, you don't recall seeing any other boats near this one last night?" Nora asked.

"I didn't say that, ma'am," Hall replied. "I didn't see any tenders. A dive boat moored close by after we'd arrived. They left again after diving the wreck."

"Constable Sommer was one of those divers," Decker pointed out.

Hall nodded. "I recognized her, sir. Her friend has shorter blonde hair with purple highlights and tattoos down her arms."

"Dat's very observant of you, Captain," Ben commented.

The captain forced a hint of a smile. "It's my job to be aware of everything going on around this yacht while I'm in command, sir."

"Yet you didn't see the black RIB with two men and a woman aboard?" Nora jabbed back.

The captain glared at her. "Correct," he finally responded curtly. "If indeed there was a black tender in the vicinity, I was unaware of it."

Ben quickly stood and thanked both Blake Decker and Captain Hall for their time. Decker took a business card from Nora and promised to email an access password and link to the pictures online as soon as the photographer had them uploaded.

As they walked along the dock, looking up at the magnificent yacht, Nora wondered how many people in the world could afford such a luxury. She knew they were in the minority, but the level of wealth displayed on the island didn't make it seem so.

"Seems like a nice enough guy," Ben said. "Helpful, at least."

"Perhaps," Nora replied. "Does your friend have a list of the crew arriving on the boat?"

"I'm sure he does," Ben replied. "It'll be in da immigration department system. Why?"

"Because the captain is either lousy at his job, or he's lying," she said, checking her watch. "He paid enough attention to describe me and AJ in detail, and yet didn't notice a RIB flying around his mega yacht."

They both stopped at the top of the dock.

Ben frowned and dug his cell phone out of his pocket. "True," he said thoughtfully. "I'll give Jaden a call and get dat list."

6

Unsure how long she'd slept, Rella stretched and realized none of it had been a dream. She was still sitting on a rock-hard floor in a stinky little room with Harper slumped against her. Her friend stirred awake and Rella noticed the thin light coming under the door had changed. Instead of a faint yellow glow from a bulb, it was the whiter light of daytime.

Harper groaned as she came to the same realization that they were still captives. "I was hoping to wake in those luxurious sheets at the Ritz-Carlton," she mumbled.

"It's morning," Rella pointed out. "I guess we'll see what they have in store for us."

"You should have told them to pound sand last night," Harper said, pushing against the filthy floor until she was sitting upright.

"I went along with everything, worried they'd kill you if I didn't. They want money; I've got it and will use every cent to get us out of here… alive."

"They know you're a billionaire," Harper said, resting her head on Rella's shoulder. "The one who brought me here took a picture and I knew they'd use it to leverage you. I can't believe I let these idiots drug me."

"I'd never leave you to fend for yourself, which could easily end in death," Rella said. Still could, she thought, and guessed Harper was thinking the same thing. "You need to behave and not do any eye poking, lest one of the men kills you. If you die, I'll hire that woo-woo woman in South Beach to set up a séance and bitch you out in the afterlife. You'll be stuck listening to us sobbing our eyes out, carrying on about what a good friend you were."

Harper leaned over and whispered, "You're crazy."

"Agreed." As much as Rella wanted to disagree, she couldn't.

"You know they can't let us go—neither of us," Harper said.

"Are we agreed that there's no provoking them unless we've exhausted our options?"

"Hate to have to admit that we're there now. I feel terrible that I was the lure to get you here." Harper tapped her head on Rella's shoulder.

"If they need money badly enough to resort to kidnapping, they'd have figured out some way to get to me, whatever it took—if it hadn't been you, then it would have been something else. It's impossible to protect yourself when you don't know someone's after you. Whatever amount they want, I'll agree to the transfer but insist that it be done in public so we can be out of there as soon as I hit the button."

Rella reminded herself to use the correct code, so it would look as if the money had been transferred but take them a while to realize they weren't able to touch a dime.

"Hate to stomp on your enthusiasm." Harper rested her bare foot on Rella's knee. "They might initially agree to whatever you demand to get what they want, but unless they're stupid, they're not going to live up to their end of the bargain."

"Then we toss more money their way to make it happen." Rella sighed, not wanting to agree with Harper.

"They haven't even tried to hide their faces, so you know there's no chance of us walking away."

"They're not the big boss," Rella assured her. "Zeus let it slip that he doesn't make the decisions, and the other one seems to take orders from him, so he's not in charge."

"I guess we'll see if big-boss-man shows his face then," Harper conceded.

"I tried to bribe Zeus and thought for a few seconds he might go for it, but then he shut down, saying he'd end up dead if he did. Wonder if he's bright enough to figure out it might happen anyway."

"What are you going to propose to the kidnappers?" Harper asked.

"I'll agree to anything as long as the two of us walk away." Rella looked around, knowing from when the door first opened that the room was minuscule. It reeked of a smell that was hard to identify. "What is this room? Is there a bathroom?"

"It's an oversized closet. As for the other, I asked the same question, and the guy pointed to a clay pot in the corner." Harper motioned to the right. "Somehow, this will all be a funny story when we get home."

"Don't do anything crazy and hack them off—play by their rules until we get our feet out the door to freedom. I know you —don't deny that you're already trying to conjure up some plan in that head of yours."

The door opened, and Apollo reappeared and waved Rella over. "Time to go."

She stood and hooked her arm around Harper's, pulling her up to stand next to her.

"Just you," he grumped.

"You want my total cooperation? Then she's coming with me. We're a package deal." Rella matched his tone.

"You're not calling the shots."

She stared him down despite the fear rippling up her spine.

Without another word, he stepped back, slamming and locking the door again.

"Weren't we supposed to be playing along?" Harper asked. "Thanks for not wanting to leave me, as I'd like to get out of this room, but not at the expense of both our lives."

Rella slid down to the floor and pulled Harper down beside her. "We're *both* getting out of here," she said with authority.

It didn't take long before the man came back. This time, he pointed his gun at them as soon as the door was open. "You're getting what you want; be prepared to pay for it." He motioned them into the other room. It had the same dirty linoleum-covered metal floors, and the only window had a tint in addition to the bars, making it difficult to see anything outside. An olive-skinned man in a dark shirt sat behind a worn desk in the middle of the back wall, irritation oozing from him. He looked up from a laptop and motioned them to sit in two metal chairs opposite him.

Rella recognized the man as the one who'd confronted her on the yacht. She searched his face, trying to recall if they'd met before last night, as she rarely forgot a face, but he was unfamiliar.

"Good to see you again, you must be Zeus," Harper said, her tone dripping with insincerity.

"Sorry if the accommodations aren't up to your standards," Zeus said, mimicking Harper's tone, then turned to Rella. "Surprises me that a woman of your means doesn't have a bodyguard. You made it too easy to gain access to you. Picking up your friend first was a last-minute idea, but a good motivator, don't you think?"

Despite Rella's background, she'd managed to keep a fairly low profile, having learned that from her parents, and had never felt unsafe going anywhere before. This trip had changed all that. "How about we come to an agreement where we both get what we want?"

"Sure. For starters, transfer fifty million into my account." He shoved a sheet of paper at Rella.

"Guessing you're aware that the amount you're requesting can't be transferred in one click, hence the multiple account numbers." She tapped the sheet in front of her. "Take me to Cayman National, where I have an account, and as a show of goodwill, I'll make a transfer of one million, which shouldn't raise any questions. You'll then take the two of us somewhere where we'll have a modicum of privacy and, once the rest of the transfers have been concluded, we can easily walk away."

"How do I know this isn't a ploy on your part designed to give you a chance to create a scene that'll bring the cops?"

"My friend and I are both eager to get back to Miami—" *And in one piece*, she left unsaid. "—and I'm not about to do anything to jeopardize either of our lives. You want fifty million, and I can make it happen. The longer this goes on, the more likely it is that our absence will be noticed and bring down the scrutiny you're looking to avoid. It's in both our interests to keep that from happening, and thus we need to come to an agreement. But before I transfer a dime, I want assurance that I'll get what I want."

"You're treating this like a friendly business deal."

"That's up to you."

7

Ben had left, promising to let Nora know once he had the crew list. She called her sergeant at West Bay station as she walked toward the dive shop building alongside the harbor.

"Sergeant Redburn," a man answered in a stern, local accent.

"It's Nora, sir. I'm following up on a lead. I'll be a few minutes late to the station."

"What case are we talkin' about here?"

"It's not an existing case, sir," she replied, trying to stay patient as she'd expected him to give her a hard time. Or at least sound like she was being patient.

"So, you mean you're just late for work."

"I met with Ben Crooks from the Joint Marine Unit at George Town harbor this morning. We're looking into a suspicious sighting from last night."

"Suspicious sighting of what?" he demanded.

Nora was now standing outside the building and the sergeant's endless questions were doing nothing more than annoying her, and making her later... for which he'd have even more questions and complaints.

"I have to go, sir, I'll fill you in when I get there. The suspect is running away."

She ended the call and waited a few moments to see if Redburn called back. He didn't, which meant she'd deferred his wrath until later. Nora pushed the door open and dodged around customers and racks of dive gear until she reached the counter.

"Constable Sommer," she introduced herself. "Do you have CCTV recorded outside the building?"

The young woman handed a waiver and a pen to a customer, then looked Nora over.

"I know you," she said in an English accent. "You're AJ Bailey's friend, yeah?"

Nora nodded. "CCTV?"

The girl seemed friendly enough and Nora recognized her from somewhere too, but she was already deep in the *dritt* with the sergeant and still had nothing to justify her suspicions.

"Oh, okay," the woman behind the counter stammered, taken aback. "We do have a camera which covers the back of the building and the dock."

"Does it reach the overflow tender dock? Where the big yacht is."

The young woman shrugged her shoulders and tried serving another customer but was now too frazzled to do both.

"Wait just a minute," she said to Nora, then apologized to the customer and disappeared into the back of the shop.

A minute later she returned. "Okay, the owner is looking at the CCTV for you. He said you can go back there."

She returned to her customer and Nora walked to the office in the rear of the shop. It was a small space with merchandise, repair items, and what appeared to be junk stacked and crammed everywhere. An older man in jeans and a golf shirt sat at a desk where a computer screen held the only section of clear space.

"What are you after, then?" the man asked. He too was English.

"Late last night that big yacht, the *DSTP*, docked. I'd like to see what happens after that."

In truth, she had no idea what she was looking for. The RIB she'd seen out by the *Kittiwake* wreck could have gone anywhere, and as it didn't belong to the yacht, she doubted it came to this dock. The passengers must have disembarked at some stage so maybe she'd spot something, but it was all a long shot at best.

The dive shop owner found the yacht approaching on his recording, and let it play as the crew secured the big boat to the dock.

"You can speed it up," Nora said, and he clicked a few times until the people ran around like old black and white movie figures.

"Normal speed," Nora urged as the passengers began walking down the dock.

They were all dressed in evening gowns and expensive looking suits. The camera only caught the back half of the yacht, but as they were leaving from the swim step at the stern, she could see everyone. Nora noticed Blake Decker was on the flybridge and waved to several of the guests. She couldn't see the captain.

The parade of guests ended, and a few crew members double-checked the lines and then could be seen milling about inside through the windows. Nora glanced at her watch and saw how late she was. When she looked back at the screen, the dive shop owner had sped the footage back up and most of the movement came from the boat itself, nudging its fenders against the dock. A few lights came on, but more went off as the crew finished cleaning and settled in for the night.

"Okay, thanks…" she began, but then saw something come into view at the back of yacht. "Slow it down."

The man returned the footage to normal speed and Nora watched a black RIB pull up to the swim step, where a man looped a line to a cleat. He was in dark clothing, similar to the figures she'd seen last night. After a few minutes, a woman came down the aft steps escorted by another man in a suit. She was wearing a white or silver dress, Nora couldn't tell which from the camera's night vision mode. She slipped off her high-heeled shoes, and the two men assisted her onto the RIB.

It was well in the distance from the camera, at night, under minimal dock and boat lights, and while it didn't look like a full-blown abduction, her body language wasn't emanating excitement either. *Or perhaps I'm projecting my own suspicion on an innocent scene*, Nora thought.

Two sightings of a black RIB with a pair of guys in dark clothes covertly transporting two different women in fancy evening wear. Nah, Nora decided, as she felt her stomach tighten, something wasn't right with all this. But her eyewitness account from last night, and the CCTV footage she'd now seen, weren't evidence of any crime. Yet.

The RIB sped off out of view to the north, around the commercial docks.

"Do you have a thumb drive I can borrow?" she asked.

The man looked at her with a frown. "Am I ever going to see it again?"

"If it means that much to you, sure," she replied, hoping he'd say no and save her the hassle.

"They don't give these things away for free, you know," he replied as he rummaged through a drawer and finally pulled out a USB stick.

Nora reached into her pocket, found a $10 CI note, and slapped it on the desk. The man grunted and began copying the CCTV file.

Back in her Jeep, Nora considered her next step. "Heading north" wasn't much of a clue as to where the RIB had gone. All the pilot had to do was stay wide of the shore and if he ran without lights again, no person or camera would have spotted him. She began driving through downtown and considered all the docks between there and Seven Mile Beach just a mile away. There weren't many and once the beach began, no docks or jetties were permitted.

Of course, the RIB could have landed anywhere on the sand, but that wasn't as easy as it sounded. The beach had a gentle slope so the little boat would bottom out in the shallow water before reaching dry land, and none of the RIB's occupants looked like they were prepared to go wading.

Nora passed by Casanova Restaurant and Rackam's on the waterfront, picturing the shoreline in her mind as she caught glances of the water between buildings. Here it was all rocky ironshore, with only a few docks that a boat could tie up and move people. She approached the Lobster Pot Restaurant building and slowed, turning into the tiny parking lot just beyond.

Parking the Jeep, she hopped out, looking at the long, narrow and slightly rickety public jetty extending into the clear water. Nora walked to the concrete patio behind the building shared by the restaurant on the upper floor and another dive operation below. She couldn't see a camera anywhere.

Wandering down the wooden topped jetty, she looked at the small, colorful fish scurrying around the concrete support posts below her. The gentle waves were the only thing distorting the view of the sandy seafloor peppered with lime-stone rocks and small coral communities.

"Hey," someone called out and Nora turned to the building.

Shading her eyes from the sun was a young woman in brightly colored yoga shorts and a dive company t-shirt. "Are you looking for something?" she asked.

Nora walked back to the patio, wondering what would prompt the woman to ask that question. A question Nora didn't have a particularly good answer for. "A black RIB was running around this area last night. I'm trying to find where it docked."

The woman nodded and chewed her lip. "I haven't seen a RIB. At least I haven't while I've been working, but we were closed after five last night. You could check with the restaurant later, when they open."

"You don't have CCTV?" Nora asked.

"We do inside, but not out here," she replied. "Don't know about them," she added, pointing to the second floor. "I'll keep an eye out for you. What's the interest in the RIB?"

"I can't say exactly," Nora said, making it sound like it was all official police business. In truth, she really couldn't say, because she didn't know. "We suspect there may have been a woman who didn't want to be on that boat."

The young woman looked at the ground and kicked her foot back and forth. "Like kidnapped? That doesn't sound good."

Nora reminded herself she didn't have time for this chitchat bullshit, but she sensed there was more the woman wasn't saying. "We'll canvas the area and find someone nearby with CCTV," she said, although doubting that was true. "If the RIB came in here, we'll figure it out."

The woman looked up; her cheeks flushed. "Of course, yeah," she mumbled.

Nora stared directly at her, unrelenting.

"Well, shit," the woman blurted. "I doubt this has anything to do with the damn boat, but come inside, I'll show you something."

Nora followed her into the dive shop. They were the only ones in there, the dive boats having just left for their morning trips. The woman reached behind the counter and pulled out a pair of sparkly silver high-heeled shoes, setting them on the glass top.

"I found these on the dock this morning," she reluctantly explained. "I almost tripped over one of them when I went down to bring the boat in from the night mooring. The other one I spotted after the sun came up. It was in the water."

"No way these were here yesterday, right?" Nora asked.

The woman shook her head.

"So sometime between 5:00 p.m. and when you arrived this morning, at what time?"

"Six thirty or thereabouts."

"They're my size," the woman said with a disgruntled look on her face. "I googled the brand. They're worth a shitload."

"Got a plastic bag?" Nora asked.

"No. We try and be plastic-free as much as possible," she replied. "You're taking them?"

"Don't touch them again," Nora ordered. "I'll get an evidence bag from my Jeep."

As she left the dive shop, Nora heard the woman swearing and mumbling something about eBay.

8

It surprised Rella when Zeus took out his phone, made a call, and spoke in a language that she didn't recognize. So eavesdropping wasn't worth the effort. He spotted that she was hanging on every word and briefly grinned, clearly realizing that she understood nothing.

As the conversation continued, Zeus appeared to struggle to keep it civil on his end. Rella could tell from the tone and body language that the man sitting in front of her wasn't the top guy. His irritation clearly showed that whatever he'd suggested had been overruled. Finally, he slammed the phone down on the desk.

"The bank it is." He took a Smith & Wesson handgun from under the desk and pointed it right between Rella's eyes. "So you know, you and I will make the trip to the bank—your friend is staying here with Apollo. Any hint that you're thinking about screwing me and you're dead. Trust me when I say it won't bother me to leave you to bleed out on the bank floor. Then I'll make a call, and your friend will die."

"That's not—"

"Shut up," Zeus barked. "Tired of hearing anything you've

got to say. If the bank run goes off without a hitch, then you'll be reunited with your friend to complete the rest of the transfer." He nodded to Apollo, said something terse, and turned back. "We'll leave after I take care of something." He shoved his chair back and stood.

Apollo yanked Harper off her chair and turned her to the door. "Get moving."

Harper jerked herself upright. Her elbow went out, barely missing Apollo's nose. He grunted when it made contact with his cheek and immediately retaliated, slapping her hard across the face. She staggered, then straightened up and glared at the man.

"Hey." Rella jumped between the two before Apollo could beat the heck out of Harper. She wouldn't go down easily, but he had bulk going for him. "You want your payday, no damaging the goods." She made eye contact with Apollo, then Zeus, making sure they both got it.

Zeus snapped at Apollo, and he stepped back grudgingly. He then lifted his gun and pointed it at Rella again. "As long as you cooperate, I won't have to use this." He waved the muzzle, opened the door, then tucked his gun in his waistband before disappearing outside.

Rella gently pushed Harper into the other room before another fight broke out. They barely got a foot inside before the door slammed and the key turned in the lock. Rella hooked her arm around Harper, led her over to the wall, and the two slid to the floor.

Harper held her face in her hands and groaned. "They're going to get their grubby hands on your money, and there's no chance we get a taste of freedom," she said through her fingers.

"You okay?" Rella winced, having seen the discoloration

beginning to form on Harper's face right after facing off with Apollo.

"Hurts like the devil," she moaned. "I should apologize for losing my mind there for a moment, but I'm not sorry. I wish I'd kicked his butt all over the room."

"Zeus found you and Apollo amusing for a nanosecond, but if it had looked like you were going to kick the man's butt, he'd have shot you—and I'm talking dead." Rella grimaced. "Not sure you realized it while being obsessed with venting your anger, but we did learn something." Rella arched her brow: *Did you catch it?* "As we suspected, neither of those men is in charge. Apollo is at the bottom of the totem pole. Zeus is second in command. The dude on the phone calls the shots."

"Got the gist from what Zeus said after that phone call, but not one other thing, since I don't speak a word of whatever that was."

"Not sure either," Rella said.

"Zeus obviously wasn't happy with how the call ended, as it was clear he wanted something different, but what?" Harper blew out a long sigh with a shake of her head. "Guessing that, if it were left to him, he'd have kept us here, placed a laptop in front of you, and coerced you however he had to, probably using me to do it, as he'd enjoy that." She flinched, clearly certain that it would involve more pain than she could handle. "Let's hope he doesn't save the fun and games until his bank account has endless zeros in it."

"I'm hoping that if I play by their rules and give them what they want, they'll reciprocate by giving us our freedom."

"Rella, when haven't you played by the rules? I feel compelled to remind you that this isn't a business deal with someone reputable. It's amazing that all the years you've been in business, you've managed to maintain that standard and somehow keep people from screwing you."

Rella could tell that Harper didn't want to tell her this might be a first for her. She didn't need telling—she was already well aware they were more likely to get screwed over than not. "Both of us need to be on our game and not do anything reckless. In case you missed it, I'm talking about you. *Do not* go off on Apollo and risk another beat-down." Rella shot Harper a stern look. "Knowing you can't see it, I'm glaring at you."

"Got it. Hoping the thought of kicking his butt and leaving him blubbering in the corner will keep my frustration at bay."

Rella laughed.

"You know…" Harper mused. "You can hardly show up to the bank barefoot in an evening dress."

"Our jailer probably hasn't given it a thought, but I'd bet the other man has it covered. Just in case, what's my excuse going to be for walking into a business barefooted?" Rella asked.

"I woke up after being drugged, my shoes were missing, and I'm not sure how it all happened," Harper said with feigned innocence.

"Not going to take your suggestion, but thanks. You know what else I'm going to need?" Not waiting for an answer, Rella told Harper, "My purse. Which is in the safe back on the yacht."

"They know you didn't come here with a purse. Whoever organized this isn't stupid and knows that you're going to need ID."

"Highly doubt that they're going to let me go back to the yacht. Wonder what they'll do when they find out my purse is locked up. Do you suppose they have access to the safe?" Rella wondered aloud.

She felt exhausted with little sleep and leaned into Harper, both using each other as a cushion. It was an awkward angle but beat stretching out on the dirty floor.

"One thing is for certain—our absence has been noticed by our husbands, and I wouldn't be surprised if they've sent out manpower to look for us," Harper said in a wistful tone.

"Though mine doesn't have the same skills as your PI husband, he'll kill those two if he gets his hands on them."

In an effort to take their minds off their situation, they then started talking about all the things they planned to do once they got off the island and finally dozed off.

The sound of the door hitting the wall jolted them awake. Apollo tossed in a plastic bag that landed at their feet. "You need to get changed, so you don't stand out," he grumbled. Then two more items came flying, one after the other.

Shocked didn't quite convey Rella's emotions as she looked down at her and Harper's purses. One of these men had figured out where their purses were and either had the combination or was adept at safe-cracking.

"What about a bathroom?" Harper shouted.

"There's a pot over there." Apollo pointed. "Or you can wait to use the portable one outside." He slammed back out, not caring what they thought of either suggestion. The door opened again. "You've got five minutes." This time, he left it open.

"Check to see if anything's missing." Rella handed Harper her purse.

Harper unzipped her evening bag and nodded. "Looks like everything's here, though there wasn't much to begin with. What about you?"

"All here." Rella held up a case with her ID in it. "Well, now we know they had access to the safes. The next question is how."

Harper grabbed the plastic bag and dumped the contents

on the floor. Two black cotton muumuus and flip-flops fell out. She jumped to her feet and held one up, then balled it up, tossed it aside, and grabbed the other one. "Thought he said he didn't want us to stand out. Then he brings us two old babe dresses—something my granny wouldn't be caught dead in."

Rella held up the two pairs of black, one-size-fits-all flip-flops. They'd work perfectly if your shoe size was a fourteen.

Harper shook her head. "Don't be surprised if your feet have a flippin' fit and plan revenge once they realize you're not outfitting them in your designer usual."

"At least they match."

They laughed.

Harper eyed the tag on one of the dresses and laughed again. "Says here big spender paid eight ninety-eight."

Rella got to her feet and turned her back to Harper. "Can you help me with my zipper?" She stepped out of her evening gown, which she left in a puddle on the floor, reached for the new dress, and pulled it over her head. She spun around. "What do you think?"

"Thinking there's room for me in there. Come over here, and let's find out." Harper grinned.

Rella ran her hands down the front of the ginormous dress, lifted one side, tied it in a knot, then slid into the flip-flops.

Harper stepped out of her dress and into the muumuu. "Not totally butt-ugly, but close."

"Too bad we can't get a picture." Rella posed.

"You two done laughing it up in here?" Apollo snarked from the doorway. "Get out here." He jabbed a finger at Rella. "The other one stays put." He pointed to the floor as if he expected Harper to sit, like a well-trained dog—he'd be disappointed. Harper balled her hands into fists and turned a glare on him meant to make him combust.

Rella stepped over to her for a quick hug and whispered,

"Behave. I feel compelled to remind you that it's better to walk away in one piece."

"Enough of the kissy-face," Apollo snapped.

With a last glance at her friend, Rella stepped out the door and heard it slam behind her as she skirted past Apollo.

"Keep walking. Out the front. Just remember that how this ends depends on you."

Rella felt the nudge of his gun in the middle of her back. Her eyes went straight to the desk, and when she didn't see the other man, she wondered where he was. Outside, she wished that Harper was standing next to her, breathing in some fresh air. It surprised her to see the boat they'd used to bring her there sitting on a trailer parked to one side of the container.

Apollo opened the back door of the SUV and grunted with impatience as she got in. After the door closed, she once again she tried the handle, to no avail. Zeus appeared out of nowhere and got behind the wheel. She turned in her seat and saw that Apollo had gone back inside.

"Where are we headed?" Rella asked. They'd agreed to take her to the bank, which was in the middle of town, but nothing would surprise her.

Instead of answering, he turned on the radio loud enough to prevent conversation—so much for talking—and drove along the dirt trail to the narrow road which led toward the taller buildings of downtown George Town.

9

Nora started her Jeep but sat there thinking instead of pulling onto the street and heading to West Bay station where she'd face a disgruntled Sergeant Redburn. Switching off the ignition, she dialed a number on her cell phone. After a few rings, a middle-aged Caymanian man answered in a business-like tone.

"Constable Sommer, good morning," Detective Roy Whittaker greeted her.

Whittaker was not only the lead detective with the Royal Cayman Islands Police Service, but also a mentor to Nora, and the man who'd offered her a position on the force. She would have to wait until she turned twenty-one years old to officially begin her detective training, but he'd already involved her in several cases and task forces when the opportunities had arisen.

Nora explained in detail what she knew so far, suggesting her next step should be a stop by the Ritz-Carlton to see if any members of the Cabot Foundation party were unaccounted for.

"That sounds reasonable," Whittaker responded. "But if

everyone is there, then I'm not sure what else we can do unless someone is reported missing, Nora."

"Yes, sir," she agreed, although at this point having found the shoes and seen the CCTV footage, she was convinced something nefarious was going on. "Would you mind getting Redburn off my arse, sir?"

Whittaker stifled a laugh. "I suspect Sergeant Redburn is just doing his job, chasing up on his errant constables, but yes, I'll let him know I've asked you to go by the hotel."

"*Takk*," she responded, then remembered to add, "Sir," before hanging up.

Nora tended to forget what she considered bullshit formalities and rank when she was focused on a case. Restarting the Jeep, she pulled onto North Church Street, which quickly became West Bay Road after the traffic lights between the gas station and one of the many waterfront cemeteries. The two-lane road ran behind the hotels, condominium complexes, and businesses fronting Seven Mile Beach where the tourist traffic made it slow going, but fifteen minutes later, Nora pulled into the valet parking for the Ritz-Carlton Hotel.

Parking off to the side, she waved off the parking attendant with a flash of her badge and marched up to the reception desk inside the impressively plush lobby.

"You have the Cabot Foundation people staying with you," she told the receptionist before the woman had a chance to begin her well-polished greeting. "I need to know if they're here."

Slightly taken aback, the woman took a moment before typing on her keyboard.

"That's correct, we have a block of twelve rooms assigned to the party."

"I know, I already told you they were staying here," Nora

said impatiently. "Are they in the rooms? I need to know if anyone is missing."

"Missing?" the woman questioned.

"Call the rooms and see if they're in there or give me the room numbers and I'll go knock on the doors."

"I'm not allowed to give out room numbers, miss," the woman stammered, completely unnerved.

"I know. That's why you're going to call each room. Now."

Overhearing the exchange, the manager appeared from an office behind the reception area, smiled at Nora, and put a hand on the receptionist's shoulder to let her know he was taking over.

"I don't have time for this *dritt*, sir," she said, trying her best to remain patient, or at least her version of patient. "We suspect someone in the Cabot Foundation group may be in trouble, so call the rooms and see who's here and who isn't."

"Certainly, we'd like to assist the police, as always, Constable Sommer," he said, reading her name from the badge pinned to her shirt. "Do you have a warrant for the rooms?"

"*Fy faen*. If I had a warrant it would have been the first thing I showed you. I don't need a warrant to call the rooms, so call the fucking rooms. Please, sir."

The manager forced a smile although he'd lost his calm demeanor and Nora could see his hands were shaking. She didn't mean to be rude or upset these people, but in her mind the situation was simple. She'd asked them to do something which inevitably they were going to do anyway, yet minutes of worthless chatter had gone by before the woman picked up the phone and began calling rooms.

It was early enough after what appeared to be a late night for the Cabot guests, that she hoped to catch everyone before they ventured out all over the island doing the things that visitors enjoyed during their stays. Every minute counted.

The manager used another phone to split the task with the receptionist, and they both spent an agonizing amount of time apologizing to the occupants of each room as one by one they woke them up. Red-faced, the receptionist finished her half of the list, and reported that everyone had answered, but Nora could hear that the final two calls the manager made went unanswered.

"Who's missing?" she asked when he stepped back.

"Mrs. Cabot and Mrs. Finn, who are in adjoining rooms," he said. "Should we be concerned?"

"You should, yes," Nora replied, setting him up for her next question. "It would be advisable to check the rooms before the maid service cleans them. We need to know if their beds were slept in."

"I can't let you in their rooms, Constable, without…"

"We've covered that already," Nora snapped, cutting him off. "Get your arse to their rooms and look for yourself!"

The manager opened his mouth to respond then thought better of it. Instead, he picked up a handheld radio and called for security. He stepped away so Nora couldn't hear the room numbers, but she gathered he was asking for a member of security to look in the rooms.

While she waited, Nora checked her email and found a link to a server with pictures from the party, forwarded by Blake Decker. Ben had also sent the crew list from the *DSTP* which had come from his friend, Jaden, at immigration. She started with the pictures, accessing them with the password Decker had included. There were hundreds of shots, all of the same theme. Various numbers of people, standing together, smiling with drinks in hand, dressed in fancy evening wear. Most of the shots were from the waist up and many included the same beautiful lady in a sparkling silver dress.

Nora guessed the woman, who she presumed was Rella

Cabot, was wearing matching shoes with the silver dress, but there again she hadn't picked up a fashion magazine in years. Scrolling through more of the pictures, she finally came across one of an older couple who didn't interest her, but in the background was a woman in a black, sequined dress, talking to Cabot. They were both far enough away in the background that they were slightly out of focus, but their feet were visible. Cabot indeed wore silver shoes to match her dress. The other lady in the black dress had strawberry blonde hair… just like the woman Nora had seen in the RIB the night before.

Nora rushed through the photographs until she found one of the two women together. They were cheek to cheek with arms around each other, giving the impression they were close friends. She held up her cell phone to the manager.

"This is Cabot, right?"

The manager studied the photograph. "It is, yes."

Before Nora had time to continue, the radio squawked and the security man's voice asked for the manager, who quickly answered.

"Ain't neither bed been slept in, best I can tell," the security guard reported.

Nora didn't waste time. "Who's the other woman?" she demanded, still holding up her phone.

"That's Harper Finn," he replied, the color having drained from his face.

"She's in the adjoining room, isn't she?" Nora pressed.

The manager nodded. "Yes. What's happened to them?" he asked, but Nora was already dialing Detective Whittaker.

She walked outside as she explained her findings, including her tenuous silver shoe connection. Sitting in her Jeep, she put the call on speaker phone and returned to her email. Opening the crew list, she found the captain's full name, Joseph Hall.

"Sir, can I send you the crew list with one name in particular to run a background check on?"

"The captain you mentioned?" Whittaker asked.

"Yes, sir."

"Give me his name, I'm at my computer."

"Joseph Hall."

Nora read off the man's US passport number and waited. She could hear one finger tapping on the keyboard and she pictured her mentor sitting at his desk, hunting and pecking.

"It appears Mr. Hall has found himself in trouble a few times," Whittaker finally said. "Two assaults, both bargained down to misdemeanors by the look of it."

"In America?" Nora asked.

"Yes. Both in Florida. His name came up in the US system but nothing from Interpol."

"Who were the victims?" she asked.

"Hmm…" the detective muttered and tapped away some more. "The first was a long time ago when he was in his twenties, but the second assault was only two years ago. A dispute over money owed to Hall. It appears he broke the man's nose instead of sending him a collections notice. The dispute was over the sale of a yacht in Miami."

"I know it's all circumstantial, sir, but I can't believe Hall didn't notice the RIB last night. I don't think that it was him on the tender, but it feels like he's covering for them."

"Okay, Nora. Let's do this," Whittaker replied thoughtfully. "I'll have someone here run background checks on the rest of the crew, while I meet you at the dock. We don't have a hope of a judge granting a search warrant based on the little we have, but if the owner is as accommodating as you found him earlier, he may let us search his boat. We can interview Hall either on the yacht, or at the station, it'll be his choice. I'll see you at the dock in ten minutes."

Nora hung up and started the Jeep with beads of sweat running in rivulets down the side of her face. Even in the shade of the tall palms lining the valet parking area, the day had warmed to a balmy eighty-eight degrees, and sitting stationary, she was cooking. The breeze across her face was a welcome relief as she sped south on West Bay Road, wishing she was in the patrol car with bright LEDs to urge the traffic aside.

Whittaker's SUV was waiting when Nora arrived, so she parked behind it with two wheels on the sidewalk. The detective stepped from his vehicle looking immaculately put together as always in his gray suit and white shirt, without a tie. It amazed Nora how he seemed oblivious to the humidity and rarely showed a single bead of perspiration.

The bright morning sun glistened off the yacht as they walked along the dock, and Nora squinted, wishing she'd kept her sunglasses on.

"Hello again, Miss Sommer," came a voice from overhead and they both paused to look up.

"Mr. Decker, this is Detective Whittaker," Nora replied, indicating the man next to her. "May we have a word with you?"

The boat owner made his way down the steps toward the stern. "Please, come aboard. Did you get the photographs?"

"*Ja*, thank you," Nora replied and let Whittaker cross the gangway first.

"Detective Whittaker," the Caymanian announced, extending his hand. "Thank you for accommodating our intrusion, Mr. Decker."

"Anything to help, Detective, and please, call me Blake. Let's get out of the sun. We can chat in the main salon."

Nora followed them both up the curved, molded steps and crossed the deck to the sliding glass doors. As before, the salon was immaculate, and the air cool, but not too cold like so many visitors kept their hotel rooms.

"We were also hoping to have a conversation with your captain if he's aboard, sir?" Whittaker said, once inside.

"Captain Hall? Is there a problem?" Decker asked.

"We have growing concerns over a couple of the guests who were aboard your yacht last night, Mr. Decker," Whittaker explained, and Nora noted he stuck to formalities. "We're hoping you and your captain can shed some light on their movements for us."

"May I ask which guests we're talking about, Detective?" Decker asked, a frown creasing his brow.

"Rella Cabot and Harper Finn," Whittaker replied. "We've just begun looking, but so far it appears no one has seen them since last night."

"My God, that's awful," Decker responded, rubbing his brow. "Rella is a friend as well as a customer. What can I do to help you?"

"Involving your captain in this discussion would be a great start, Mr. Decker. Perhaps you could ask him to join us?"

The boat owner's face dropped. "I'm afraid I don't know where he is right now, Detective. He left the yacht shortly after Constable Sommer's earlier visit. He didn't tell me where he was going."

10

Harper gritted her teeth as the door closed and listened to see if Apollo locked it. Which he, of course, did. She began grumbling and threw herself down in the corner, her eyes glued to the door.

"I'm not as optimistic as Rella about getting out of this container in one piece," she mumbled to herself. *I'm supposed to behave? Why? The heck with that*, she thought as her anger escalated at everything that had happened. *If I make a run for it, Apollo will be hot on the phone to Rella, wanting to know where I could have gone and spouting threats. Instead of answering his questions, I'd hope she'd also go on the run... if she can.*

Harper took a deep breath, refusing to think about all the ways this new idea of hers could go wrong. She went to the doorway and lay on the floor, stretching out across the opening. Sucking in as much air as her lungs could hold, she yelled "help" over and over. After about the fifteenth time, when her voice was ready to give out, the door was thrown open. Apollo tripped over her and hit the floor.

Harper managed to roll away, scramble to her feet, and get out of the room, slamming the door behind her. Once in the main office, she couldn't believe her luck when she saw that the front door had been left open. A foot from freedom, Apollo grabbed her arm. The two danced around, and she kneed him in the groin. He doubled over, and she shot outside. *Rella's going to kill me.*

It seemed like a good idea until Harper realized that she had no idea which way to go. When in doubt… She eyed the row of trees at the far end of the buildings. She was within a foot of disappearing into the foliage when Apollo crashed into her and sent her flying to the ground. The pain was unbelievable as she struggled to catch her breath.

"Bitch," he hissed in her ear. He grabbed a handful of Harper's hair and jerked her to her feet.

It hurt so bad, Harper was surprised he hadn't ripped a clump from her scalp.

Apollo spun her around, anchoring her back to his chest, his foul breath blowing against the side of her face. "Did you really think you'd get away?" he asked with a sly undertone. "Thinking I should kill you now; what do you think?" He pressed the muzzle of his gun under her jaw.

"I'll behave, I promise," she gasped, planning nothing of the sort. She wasn't about to go down without a fight.

He chuckled humorlessly in her ear. "You haven't so far. Why would I believe you now?" Apollo twisted her around and sent her flying. This time, she landed on her butt, gravel digging into her skin. He whipped out a pair of handcuffs and dangled them in front of her.

Getting cuffed can't happen. She inched backward.

"How about I leave your bloodied remains out here among the trees? 'Hey look, I tried, but she wouldn't stop, and she was getting away.' Sounds good, don't you think?" His lips twisted into a mean smile. "They won't be happy you're dead, but they'll see it as better than you escaping." He jerked his head. "Get the hell over here."

Harper rose slowly to her feet, hoping against hope for an opportunity to disappear into the row of trees. The branches would conceal her, hopefully buying enough time to find a way out the other side.

A rustling noise caught both their attention.

When Harper spotted two iguanas chasing one another up the tree trunk, she struggled to keep from laughing, giddy with the realization that they'd given her a diversion. No way was she getting cuffed and dragged back to that dingy room. He was too close for her to get away, so while his attention was diverted, she launched herself on him and put all her weight into slugging him in the throat.

Apollo made an enraged sound, grabbing his throat with one hand and her with the other. He'd dropped the cuffs and the gun.

Harper hit him again.

His fist caught her in the face.

She screamed. He grabbed her again and tightened his hold.

Harper fought like a wildcat and managed to struggle out of his grasp. He whirled her around and sent her flying into the trunk of a tree. She scrabbled to her knees and crawled away.

"You're not going anywhere," he bellowed and launched himself on top of her.

They rolled in the weeds and dirt, fighting for control.

Harper used all her strength and managed to roll on top of him and wrap her hands around his neck; the sound of him choking didn't slow her any.

His fist landed in her gut, then the side of her face.

Harper hissed, her breath driven out of her. She was losing

the fight, and she knew it. She'd seen the weapon Apollo had dropped, she reached out and grabbed it. The two fought over the gun, and it went off, which surprised him more than her. She'd kick herself later for dropping it as she managed to get to her feet and disappear into the trees.

Branches scraped her arms and weeds scratched at her legs as she crisscrossed through the trees, not sticking to a straight path. Her ninety-nine-cent shoes had had enough of the fun, and the v-strap on one broke.

Apollo screamed her name over and over as he got closer, and she knew it was only a matter of minutes before he'd be on top of her. She threw herself behind a shorter tree and sank into the undergrowth, sticking her fist in her mouth so she wouldn't squeal if a bug crawled on her or, worse yet, bit her. She realized he'd slowed his search. He had to have noticed that he could no longer hear her crashing through the woods. She hoped he thought she'd gotten away.

He took a couple of shots into the woods, and not even her fist could smother the scream when she felt a bullet breeze by her.

The next thing Harper knew, Apollo was on top of her and dragging her up by her hair again, not making much headway though the pain was excruciating. He hooked his arm through hers, dragged her out of the trees, lifted her slightly, and kicked her onto the grassy strip.

He pointed his gun at her face. "There's no reason to prolong the fiction that you're walking out of this still breathing. It'll be my pleasure to pull the trigger."

Harper waited for the blast, but it didn't come. Instead, he slammed his gun into the side of her head, and everything went dark.

11

Nora walked alongside Detective Whittaker as they left the *DSTP* and Blake Decker, ambling down the dock with the enormous yacht next to them. The owner had tried calling his captain's cell phone without any luck reaching Hall. They also called Rella Cabot's number but that had gone directly to voicemail. Decker told them he'd seen and thanked Rella after returning to the harbor and had left her to say goodnight to her guests. He couldn't recall seeing Harper Finn much during the evening, but he'd been busy schmoozing potential yacht buyers.

"We don't have enough to put out a BOLO on Hall," Whittaker said as they reached their vehicles. "I'll send a note over to immigration, so they'll notify us if he tries to fly out, and he just left his best means of departing by sea. He can't stay hidden for long."

"As long as Decker lets us know if he returns to the ship," Nora pointed out.

"Which I believe he will," Whittaker responded. "And remember, he's nothing more than a person of interest based on his attitude and priors. That's thin evidence to go anywhere with."

"Plus, he took off after we came by this morning," Nora added, her gut feeling about the man getting stronger.

"Or, he went to visit a friend, buy souvenirs, or tour the Turtle Centre," Whittaker reminded her. "He may simply have forgotten to mention anything to Decker."

Nora wasn't buying it for a moment and was sure the detective would feel the same way if he'd met the captain. She'd also learned that Whittaker was very good at hiding his suspicions until proof confirmed his leanings. Knowing Nora was already sure Hall was up to something, it would be like him to remain strictly unbiased in front of her, even if he felt the same way.

The cell phone in Nora's pocket rang and she checked the caller ID. It was Sergeant Redburn. She couldn't dodge him all day, so she answered the call.

"Constable Sommer."

"Don't make out you don't know who's calling, missy," he barked. "Are you done runnin' around playin' detective, now?"

Nora looked up at Whittaker wondering what their next move would be. Back to her beat in West Bay for her was most likely until something else surfaced.

"I'm leaving George Town now," she said, hoping Whittaker would override that plan.

"I doubt that," Redburn snapped back. "If you'd bin listenin' to your radio, you'da heard dat black RIB you bin lookin' for bin spotted. Leastways, *a* black RIB. Can't say for sure it's da one you wanted but call into Central and find out."

In her haste, Nora forgot to thank the sergeant before hanging up and grabbing her handheld radio she'd left clipped to the dashboard of her Jeep. She hailed Central and quickly explained what was going on to a puzzled looking Whittaker while she waited for a response.

"We'll take my car," Whittaker said, unlocking the SUV.

Nora's radio sparked to life at the same time her phone vibrated in her hand. "PC277, this is Central. Texting you coordinates now. Zulu 4 is at location. Over."

Nora leapt into her Jeep, started the engine, and keyed the radio mic. "Central, this is PC277. Received message. Over." As she put the CJ-7 in gear, she shouted to Whittaker, "Follow me! If I leave the Jeep, they'll tow it!"

As the detective climbed into his SUV, Nora clicked on the coordinates in the text message which open the location in her maps app. Recognizing the street, which wasn't far away, she pulled out in front of oncoming traffic with a wave of her hand, backed up, and made a brisk three-point turn to a chorus of horn honks. In the rearview mirror she noticed flashing red-and-blue lights from Whittaker's Range Rover, which immediately silenced the horn honkers, although they probably thought he was chasing her.

Speeding down North Church Street, Nora overtook several tourist vehicles, surprising the sightseers as they gazed around at the little shops and restaurants by the water. At the traffic lights by the cemetery, instead of waiting for a green light to make a right turn with the other cars in line, she swung hard right into the gas station. The Jeep bounced across the sidewalk and swerved around a startled man at the pumps. At the far side, she made sure not to hit an oncoming van then cut into traffic heading west on Eastern Avenue, earning another loud honk of the horn. Just past Kirk Marine, Nora made a left onto Courts Road and slowed down as she approached the pin on the map where a patrol car sat parked by the side of the road.

Nora parked behind them, jumped out of the Jeep and

jogged to the driver's side window. By the time she reached them, Whittaker pulled in behind her Jeep with his lights extinguished.

"Hey," she greeted the two George Town constables in the car, neither of whom she recognized. "Where's the RIB?"

The two local policemen looked at Nora's blonde hair spilling from beneath her hat and grinned.

"Dis is da famous Constable Sommer we bin hearin' about, huh?" the driver said. "I hear you da boss of ole Jacob Tibbetts?"

They both began laughing, but quickly stopped when Detective Whittaker walked up next to Nora.

"The RIB?" Nora demanded.

Both men pointed to a yellow shipping container at the edge of a large parcel of unused scrubland, cleared of trees. On the far side of the rectangular steel box sat a boat trailer carrying a black-and-gray rigid inflatable boat. Nora wished she'd had time to snap a picture out by the wreck, but she doubted the black RIB would have shown up in the dark. Foraging in her pocket, she pulled out the thumb drive from the dive shop and handed it through the window.

"Bring up the CCTV video on here," she told the constable, and he plugged the thumb drive into the USB port of the patrol car's dash mounted laptop, after flipping it over several times to align the USB plugs.

She gave them the timestamp from the note she'd made and after dragging the cursor to the right spot, they all leaned in and watched the RIB arrive at the stern of the *DSTP*. Nora looked back and forth from the screen to the boat, which was a hundred yards away, paying attention to the profile of the helm station, seat, and outboard motor.

"Looks da same to me," the constable in the driver's seat said.

Nora waited a little longer until the woman was hustled aboard, and the RIB left again. The footage was grainy, with the green tint of night vision, but she could make out white lettering across the upper part of the black motor, although the word was too blurry to decipher. She looked across the grassy expanse at the RIB by the container. The outboard engine was black with "Suzuki" in block capitals across the side of the upper cowling.

The container itself had been converted into an office of some description, with a barred window, door, and air conditioner on the roof. Apart from the boat on the trailer, there were no other vehicles, nor any signs of life.

Nora looked at Whittaker. "That's a match."

He nodded. "You two wait here and watch in case anyone bolts or shows up. Hold anyone who arrives."

"Yes, sir," the men responded in unison.

"Think there's a second entrance?" Nora asked, only able to see one side and the long front face of the yellow container.

"Those office conversions don't usually," he replied as they both started down the rough gravel driveway. "But who knows what this one was built for."

As they neared the steel structure, sitting alone at the edge of the lot, Nora split off to circle around the back. The grass was longer behind the container, and she trod carefully to stay quiet and not twist an ankle on the uneven terrain. The air conditioner whirred above her and from somewhere came the low drone of a generator.

The back side was the uninterrupted corrugated metal form of a normal container, without doors or windows, and she found the far end the same when she completed the loop and joined Whittaker by the door.

She shook her head, indicating there weren't any other

exits, then pointed to the door, which was pushed to, but not closed.

"Police," Whittaker announced. "Is anyone inside?"

Met with silence, he pulled the door handle, letting the door swing outward. Nora stayed close to the building, looking inside to their right, while Whittaker scanned to their left. Seeing nobody, Nora stepped inside with her hand on her Taser, announcing their presence again.

"Main room clear," she said just loud enough for the detective to hear and moved to the right where a door lay open to a second room.

Taking her flashlight from her duty belt she swept the beam around the dark, windowless room, ready to step back if necessary, but the room appeared empty, at least of people and furniture.

"Clear," she called out, and relaxed, playing the light around, looking for details.

The room was indeed bare, apart from a clay pot in the corner, and a pile of clothes in the middle of the floor. She walked over and shone her light on one black and one silver evening gown, next to a pair of black stiletto heels.

"I think you can put out a BOLO for the two women, sir," Nora said, returning to the main room and inspecting the back of the door to the dark room. "Their clothes are in there, and I'd say by the stinky pot in the corner, and the locks on the door, they were being held against their will."

Whittaker was looking around a steel desk in the corner of the main room, finding nothing in the single drawer which he opened with a gloved hand. A matching steel chair sat behind the desk and two more off to the side near the lone window. A simple light fixture screwed to the ceiling lit the room, its wire running to and down the far wall, disappearing into the grubby linoleum covered floor.

"There's power," Whittaker noted.

"I heard a generator running out the back somewhere," Nora replied, looking up at the vent in the ceiling losing a battle with the hot air coming in through the open door. "Why would you leave the generator and AC running, then not close the door?"

"Careless, perhaps?" Whittaker replied as Nora stepped outside and looked around.

"Or rushed," she commented, walking away in the opposite direction from the driveway to the road.

The grass was coarse, and the ground riddled with limestone pebbles among the dirt, like much of the island's barren soil. The terrain made it hard to see footprints or tracks, but she walked in an arc, looking for signs of movement. Tire tracks led to and from the boat trailer, and the grass and weeds were trodden down from activity, but she couldn't make out any distinct boot prints.

About to give up and return to Whittaker, who was calling in orders to Central, Nora noticed something shiny in the grass. She crouched down, and slipping on a nitrile glove from her pocket, picked up a pair of handcuffs.

12

Harper swam slowly up out of the blackness, her head throbbing like a drum. She groaned.

"Shut the hell up," a man's voice growled in her ear. "If I'm going to end up with a bullet in my back, then so are you. You first."

Feeling the muzzle of a gun against her temple, Harper managed to swallow back any more sounds. She took note of her surroundings, realizing she was lying on her side in foot-high foliage, her head pounding and sunlight stabbing her eyes as she struggled to remember what had happened. "What are we—?"

Apollo clamped his hand over her mouth. "This is as far as I could drag you, and we need to lie low while they snoop around."

"What's—"

He stuck the muzzle of his gun in her mouth.

Afraid to move an inch, she tried to telegraph that she'd cooperate. Unsure whether he got the message, she concentrated on not moving.

Apollo leaned into her face. "Are you going to cooperate, or do we end it here?" The man was enjoying himself too much.

To Harper's relief, he removed the gun from her mouth. She rubbed her lips. "What's going on?" she whispered. The last thing she remembered was the pain in her head and everything going black. She didn't have a clue how long she'd been out. There wasn't anywhere on her body that wasn't screaming in pain.

"The cops are snooping around the container. I'd like to know why, but I can assure you that they're not going to find anything of interest," Apollo said with confidence.

Harper thought about their dresses on the floor in the back room but didn't correct him. She peeked through the long grass and saw a tall, slender blond policewoman searching the ground outside the container. The woman was the most unlikely looking islander Harper could have imagined. More akin to a Scandinavian athlete wearing a uniform. She watched the female cop pick up the handcuffs.

Apollo growled and squeezed Harper's cheeks... hard. "That's your fault."

She eased backward out of his hold. "I said I'd cooperate, and I'm not going back on my word. What do you need me to do?"

He pointed to their left, where a fence ran along the side of what appeared to be an industrial park. They must be the warehouses Rella had mentioned when she'd described their surroundings last night, she thought. Harper had still been too woozy from the drugs to take in anything when they'd brought her to the dark room.

"Crawl that way and stay low," he ordered. "And if you make a sound, it'll be the last thing you do."

Harper looked where he was pointing and spotted a hole in the fence where someone had pinned the wire back. She crawled in the direction he'd indicated but stopped after a few yards.

"There's water," she hissed. "You planning to pole vault across?"

"What the hell," he groaned and wriggled up alongside her.

Before them was a steep embankment leading to a canal, which ended at the field to their right. If the cops hadn't been watching, they could have easily walked around the end. To the left, the water extended as far as they could see into more woods.

"Get going, and stay low," Apollo ordered.

Harper looked at him as though he was mad. "Through that?" she whispered, looking at the mucky brownish green canal. It was only five yards wide, but she had no idea how deep it was or who lived there. Being from Florida, she knew better than to go paddling in soupy creeks.

"Yes, in there," he replied through gritted teeth. "Slide down the bank and wade across."

"You go first; I'll follow," she said, hoping to see her kidnapper dragged away by a gator.

He gave her a hard shove, and she slithered over the edge of the bank, catching herself before she hit the water.

"All right, all right. Give me a minute." She looked back up the slope at Apollo. "You know they're called the Cayman Islands, right? And you know a caiman is a type of alligator… I doubt that's a coincidence."

Apollo waved his gun at her. "Get going. Now!"

Harper let out a long sigh and dipped a bare toe in the warm water, watching closely for anything stirring. She heard Apollo sliding down the muddy slope behind her, and before she could ready herself, he bashed into her, knocking her forward into the canal. Harper managed to get a leg out in front of herself and stayed upright as she splashed into the water, which was only two feet deep.

"Keep quiet, damn it!" Apollo grouched.

"You shoved me, you Neanderthal," she retorted.

She shuffled across the mucky, branch-and-foliage-strewn canal in her bare feet, grimacing with every step. Things brushed, scraped, and grazed her ankles with each step, but she forced herself to imagine that the water was free of ugly, biting creatures. At the far side, she clawed her way up through the long grass and reeds until she could sit on the top of the embankment and watch Apollo cross behind her.

Harper thought about running while he was still in the water, but the gun in his hand had all the reach he needed to catch her, and while his subsequent arrest would be satisfying, it wouldn't mean much if she was shot dead.

Apollo clambered up the bank and pointed to the fence. "Through there."

Deciding she'd behave for now... until another opportunity presented itself, Harper ducked through the hole in the fence. If she did escape, what would happen to Rella? Her friend was the one with the money, so they weren't likely to hurt her. Yet. But Harper was being used as the incentive for Rella to play along. Comply, or we'll shoot your bestie. She needed to escape and get to the police... who were only a hundred yards away.

"This is all your fault," Apollo grumbled as he stood up and shook Harper by the scruff of the neck.

She jerked out of his hold, rubbing the back of her neck. "We both know I wasn't the one who called the cops."

Apollo grunted and looked around. "How do we get out of here without being seen?" he mumbled.

A wolf whistle rent the air. Harper turned toward the warehouses and saw that the end unit one row over had their door rolled up, and several men stood in the opening. A couple of them waved and continued to whistle.

"Ignore them and keep moving." Apollo prodded. "They wouldn't think you were hot if they knew what a pain in the ass you are."

Hearing another whistle, Harper took off running toward the men, waving her arms and yelling, "Help!"

She braced herself for the excruciating pain of a bullet ripping through her flesh, but it never came. Only the sound of Apollo's feet pounding after her.

She managed to stay just ahead of him all the way to the men. "I don't want to see that man anymore, and he's not taking no for an answer," she pleaded as they stepped toward her.

"Dis fella, he bothering you?" the first man asked. He was a brawny, dark-skinned local in cutoff pants and a tank top. He and his friends put themselves between Harper and Apollo.

"You don't want to get involved in this, guys," Apollo said, but Harper noticed he'd tucked his gun away.

"Down da end, miss," the last man to come out of the warehouse said. "Go to da road and turn right. We bin seeing police all over da place."

"Can I just call the police from here, please?" she asked, but as the words left her lips, the herbal and woody odor of marijuana reached her nose.

"Not 'ere, miss. We don't need no 5-0 round 'ere."

"Okay, thank you," she told him and began to walk away, weighing her options.

The group of locals had made a semicircle around Apollo, and no one was watching her. She could slip inside the open warehouse and find a phone, but the guys had just rescued her, so that didn't seem fair. The other option was to head in the direction the man had suggested and find the police. Choosing the latter, she began jogging along the ends of the buildings, making for the road. Looking back, she was glad to see that Apollo was between the buildings and couldn't see where she was going.

Her beaten and cut bare feet felt like they were on fire from the hot concrete, and she quickly realized she couldn't make it to the road without something to cover them. Clinging close to a building, she stood in the shade and looked down the next alleyway. The door to a unit was not quite closed.

Trying to make minimal contact with the ground, Harper hopped over to the door and went inside what appeared to be a basic office. She wondered where the owner was... until she noticed that the door had been jimmied open. *Great*, she thought, *I ran from a kidnapping straight to the scene of a break-in.* She made a mental note not to touch anything... except for the phone. All she had to do now was call the police and they'd come running. Surely, she was far enough from the guys who'd helped her by now that the cops wouldn't hassle them. Except there was no phone, just a bare wire on the desk.

"Now what?" she mumbled to herself. *I'd rather be tucked up in here than in Apollo's grasp. But for how long?* She eased down to the floor and stretched out her legs, wiggling her toes and feet, happy they hadn't given up on her and fallen off.

Harper tipped her head back against the wall and closed her eyes. Her optimism at her cobbled-together plan was beginning to annoy her as she reminded herself, she didn't know exactly where she was or precisely where she was going. What she did figure was that it wouldn't take long for Zeus, and therefore Rella, to be told that she'd disappeared. *Maybe Rella could make a run for it herself?*

It then dawned on her that Apollo couldn't see her, but by

the same token, she couldn't see him. She had no idea where he was. The locals had probably sent him on his way, and he'd now be hunting her again. Meanwhile, thanks to her bloodied feet, she'd had to hole up for now, but would have to make a move at some point... and be the prey once more.

13

More police cars arrived and the entry to the scrublands was beginning to turn into a parking lot.

"*Fy faen*," Nora muttered to herself, watching a handful of constables walk toward her and Whittaker.

"I know," Whittaker said, stepping from the container office to join her outside. "It's frustratingly time-consuming organizing a group, but running into the woods alone is risky and an individual is easier to evade."

"They'll be long gone, sir," she complained.

"You mean, you'd be long gone," he said with a grin.

She couldn't argue his point. Since joining the police force Nora had been amazed how stupid the average criminal turned out to be. Predictable and unimaginative, unlike the skills she'd learned from spending several years travelling the world as a teenage runaway. But they weren't all dumb. She'd also encountered a few who were terrifyingly smart and devious. She hoped these kidnappers weren't the clever variety.

"Ladies and gentlemen," Whittaker announced as the constables neared. "We'll start by sweeping the woods behind us. Spread out, form a line, and keep your eyes peeled. We're looking for two Caucasian women in their thirties, and we know of at least two men who we believe apprehended them. We're thin on descriptions for the men, beyond Caucasian and larger build. Question anyone you come across, regardless of description, and ask if they've seen anything or anyone suspicious." He pointed to the woods. "Let's go, and stay in communication with each other, report sightings over the radio."

The uniformed men and women, ten in all, moved toward the trees, fifty yards from the container. The two men who had spotted the RIB remained on watch near the entry to the field, and Nora waited for Whittaker to finish a phone call he'd made after sending the searchers on their way.

"I have the helicopter on standby," he said, after hanging up. "Can't justify putting the bird in the air without at least a sighting."

"They must have a vehicle," Nora commented. "So, either they're driving who knows where and had already abandoned this place, or they were split up and whoever was left here has run. If our guys who spotted the RIB had flushed them out, they should have seen them. Certainly a vehicle leaving, as there's only one way out of this field by car."

Whittaker scanned the terrain thoughtfully. "All good observations. It's the door and generator that bother me."

"And the clothes," Nora agreed. "Why leave obvious evidence to be found? If they'd thrown a cover over the RIB, we'd never have found it. Plus, the handcuffs."

"It's almost as though the women escaped," Whittaker proposed. "But why would they ditch their clothes? And why wouldn't they run straight for help? There's a petrol station a quarter of a mile away."

Nora stepped into the container, turned around, and jumped out, running in the direction she'd found the handcuffs, now marked with a small orange flag. She slowed to a stop and looked ahead, slowly shifting her focus from the woods to the open scrub to her left. *Too much open terrain.*

Pivoting to her right, Nora looked at the ten-foot-high wire fence dividing the field from a small industrial complex. Only twenty yards away, the fence turned ninety degrees right along the side of the businesses, parallel to a drainage canal.

"If I ran, I would have gone for the road if I could. But if that wasn't an option and I needed cover, I'd go that way," she said, pointing to the canal.

Whittaker followed her direction. "So, you're saying I just sent all our manpower into the wrong woods?"

"*Ja,*" she replied. "But you and I can cover this direction."

Whittaker paused a beat, weighing their options, before radioing the two constables at the entrance and telling them to keep an eye on the container.

"They won't be back there," Nora said, reinforcing what she assumed he was thinking.

"If Cabot and Finn are looking for safety, I want to make sure we're giving them as many options as possible," Whittaker responded, then strode keenly toward the canal. "Come on then, let's see if Norwegians make good trackers."

The canal didn't look deep but was a far cry from the clear turquoise ocean less than half a mile from where they stood. The water was still and the banks on either side quite steep, lined with long grass and weeds.

"Which side would you try if you were running?" Whittaker asked.

Nora studied the tall grass giving way to low, thick shrubs and trees on the left bank, then the narrow embankment between the industrial park fence and the canal. Something caught her eye twenty yards along the fence.

"I'd use the cover of the trees on the left," she replied, "and that's where I'm sure they went."

"Okay," Whittaker complied, and began moving to the left.

"But then someone crossed the canal and went into the warehouse place," Nora added, stopping the detective in his tracks. "See the hole in the fence," she added, pointing to a small section of wire folded back.

"Your young eyes are keener than mine," Whittaker muttered, changing directions. "But if one of us has to go in that dirty water, I'm pulling rank on you."

Nora grunted and nimbly jogged along the embankment, knocking high weeds and small branches aside. When she arrived at the gap in the fence, she studied the ground. There were recent muddy marks where feet had climbed the embankment from the water. Whittaker reached her and examined the scrapes and gouges.

"Two people?"

"*Ja*," Nora agreed. "One with big boots. The other one is smaller, and I don't see any sole prints."

Nora dropped to her knees and scurried through the cut in the fence, holding it back as far as it would go as Whittaker grunted and groaned as he followed, snagging his jacket on the wire.

"I'm too old for this," he grumbled as he stood up on the concrete slab surrounding the long, narrow warehouses.

Nora pointed to the ground where muddy, wet prints led toward the alley between the first two buildings before the tracks faded, as the dirt must have cleaned from the runners' feet.

"The prints are over one another," Nora said, continuing in the direction the prints had been going.

"That doesn't necessarily mean one was chasing the other," Whittaker pointed out. "Perhaps they were walking in line."

Nora knew he was right, and it was another reminder not to jump to conclusions, but why would two people choose to run through the canal? Taking a minute longer, they could have walked around the end where the water stopped at the field. She remained silent and watched an old pickup truck full of local workers pull out from between buildings farther down the row.

One of the men in the bed of the truck touched two fingers to his own eyes before pointing at her. She figured he was being a smart arse, telling her he was watching what the police were doing, but then he lifted his hand up high, indicating something or someone tall. He then pointed to the buildings all around them.

"Stop! Wait!" she yelled, but the pickup disappeared from view and continued out of the industrial park.

Nora used her radio to call the two constables at the entrance to the scrubland, and she and Whittaker waited for them to stop the truck so they could further question the men. Finally, they radioed back and said no truck came their way.

"Where the hell did they go?" Nora fumed.

Whittaker shook his head. "Maybe the apartments behind the industrial park?" he proposed.

"That street ends there, right?" Nora asked, pointing to Courts Road at the far side of the warehouses, the street which they'd used to reach the scrubland. The same road the two constables were parked on and surely would have seen anyone come and go.

"The paved road ends after the apartments, yes," Whittaker confirmed, then thought a moment. "But I don't know if there's a dirt trail to the bypass beyond," he added. "Sometimes the locals clear a path to the main road if it makes getting about easier. What was the guy in the back of the truck signaling you about?"

"*Fy faen*," she cursed under her breath as she pieced it together. "He was telling us to watch for a tall man."

"Hmm," Whittaker grunted, and followed Nora down the alley between the first pair of buildings. At the end, the fence separated the industrial estate from the scrubland where she could see the back of the RIB on its trailer and the container office. A generator hummed from a patch of long grass on the other side of the fence, with a power line snaking its way toward the small metal building.

Whittaker walked up next to her, and they both turned to their left, looking down the back row of the warehouse buildings. At the far end, a tall figure in black trousers and a dark shirt ducked out of view. Nora immediately took off at a sprint, her long, lean legs covering ground quickly. As she ran, Whittaker's voice became fainter, but she could hear enough to know, he was barking orders into his phone. He'd decided it was time to have eyes in the sky.

14

Twenty minutes earlier…

"You surprised me—I expected you to try to alert the authorities," Zeus said as he grabbed Rella's elbow and hung on tight as they exited the bank, then steered her down the sidewalk. "There was a minute or two when I thought the bank president wasn't going to go through with the transaction."

Your leering at her and staring down her top wasn't helpful. "It made it easier that you chose a local bank to receive the funds."

After having given Rella's cheap dress and shoes a once-over, the bank manager's surprise was evident when she pulled up her bank balance. After that, her chilly stare at being requested to facilitate the transaction had warmed some. When they finished, the woman pushed a business card into Rella's hands and gushed, "If there's anything else you need…"

"I was prepared to leave a pile of dead bodies behind. Happy you didn't make me do that."

"I gave you my word that I'd cooperate." *How many times had she told him that, yet he needed another reminder?* She held back a disgruntled sigh. "Now, how about you showing some good faith? I want to wait at the pastry shop over there and indulge in a good cup of coffee while you get Harper."

His narrowed eyes and loud snort let her know it wasn't happening.

"You don't like that idea? Then have Apollo bring her here. Do I need to remind you that we agreed on handling the rest of the transaction in a public place?"

"Plans have changed. The way I see it, we've got your friend and thus hold all the cards." *Now, don't we?* on his face.

Zeus opened the SUV's passenger door and gave her a hard shove, and she stumbled into the seat. He slammed the door and walked around to the driver's side. Well, at least she'd graduated to the front seat.

As he pulled away from the curb, Rella asked, "If you're not going to honor your agreement, then why should I cooperate?"

His lips pulled into a tight line.

"Do you have any intention of letting us go? Or are you just full of hot air, saying what you know I want to hear?"

"We can finish this deal at the office without worrying about unwanted eyes," he growled back.

Rella stared out the window and saw that Zeus wasn't taking the same route back that he'd used when taking her to the bank. She assumed it was so that if she somehow got away, which was looking less and less likely, she wouldn't have a clue where she was.

"If you're planning an escape route…" He laughed.

"I'm not the one going back on my word," Rella struggled

not to snap. She felt like she was running out of time to get him to live up to his side of the agreement.

They were back on a familiar road, and Zeus signaled, began turning left onto the little street to the lot with the container office, then suddenly veered back onto the road they'd been on. A hundred yards ahead, he swung into a Blackbeard's Beer, Wine, and Spirits parking lot on the left. Pulling around the side of the large building, he nosed the SUV up to the fence fronting the road and stared across the scrubland toward the container.

Rella now realized why he'd made the detour. Multiple police cars were parked next to the container, and another guarded the entrance to the field. She couldn't see anyone except for the two cops in the car by the entry, but the door to the container was open. *Where the heck was Harper?*

"Did you forget to lock the door?" she asked, knowing it would irk her captor.

"Shut it with the questions," Zeus growled, pulling his phone out of his pocket and scrolling across the screen. He read a text and his face grew red with anger. Rella was sure he was about to throw his phone, but then he seemed to think better of it and dialed a number. "Where the hell are you?"

Rella guessed that he was talking to Apollo.

She couldn't make out the answer, but his eyes darkened, and he looked ready to spit nails. He began ranting something indecipherable. When the call ended, he threw his phone in the cup holder.

"Where the hell did your friend go?" he asked, turning, and leaning over, getting inches away from Rella's face.

"Harper's gone?" Rella asked, her eyes darting back to the container. "I've been with you every second since we left this place, so how could I know anything?" She hoped Harper got away and would rain down hell on these two. Or that she already had, and hence the police. From the look on Zeus's face, he was thinking the same thing.

"Was this some plan that the two of you cooked up?"

"How is that possible when we haven't been together for hours and neither of us is familiar with the area? You need to calm down; Harper wouldn't do anything stupid." Rella knew she would, but he could find that out on his own. She looked down and bit back a smile.

"What are the cops looking for? Who called them? They don't show up for no reason," Zeus muttered under his breath. "Your damn friend has caused this mess." He groaned, and this time, it was loud and practically rattled the windows. "If the cops don't have her, and I find her first…"

Rella dreaded whatever he'd left unsaid and hoped Harper had already found her way to the police. "You should call the boss and let him know what's going on," she said, to see his reaction.

He clenched his jaw.

"He's the one calling the shots—he won't like being the last to know."

"Shut up," Zeus said, rage in his eyes. "When I want your opinion, I'll ask. Don't hold your breath waiting for that to happen. Not another word out of you."

His phone rang, and this time, he unleashed an unrelenting tirade before hanging up and slamming it down in the cup holder. Rella guessed things weren't going well on Apollo's end.

———

Harper scanned the alley outside the office but couldn't see anyone. *Was Apollo staying hidden and waiting for her to move?* She had no way of knowing and couldn't stay there all day.

Zeus and Rella would surely be back by now, and with a bit of luck, they'd run slap bang into the police at the container.

Harper knew she needed to get herself to the policemen she'd seen, which either meant going back through the hole in the fence or finding the entrance to the industrial park. Without running into Apollo. Her body ached and her head throbbed, reminding her what lay in store if he found her again. The other alternate was finding a phone.

She heard the sound of a vehicle getting closer and pressed her face to the window to see the wider road running by the ends of the warehouses. A pickup truck rolled by, packed full with what looked like her friendly saviors.

"Here goes nothing," she muttered to herself and opened the door a crack.

She listened but couldn't hear anything beyond air conditioners and distant traffic. Harper slipped out of the office and made her way to the end of the building, staying tight against the wall. At the road which the pickup had left down, she peeked both ways. To her left, a hundred yards and several buildings away, was the hole in the fence. To her right, three more warehouses before the fence that ran along the road, leading to the scrubland and the container.

Hearing footsteps behind her, Harper ducked around the corner and took a quick look back down the alley. Someone had run along the path at the opposite end of the buildings, but she didn't get a good look. *Maybe a white shirt?* She got the impression it was a woman, but it could have been her mind playing tricks.

Not wanting to risk running into the wrong person, she hobbled across the road to the row of buildings on the other side, continuing until she reached the pathway behind them. Another fence separated her from several apartment buildings and for a moment, she considered scaling the wire, but in bare feet and the stupid dress, Harper figured she'd end up snagged and hanging like a rag doll for Apollo to find.

Turning to her right, she jogged along the back of the buildings, wincing with each step, carefully checking the first alleyway before crossing. At the second gap, she glanced around the corner and saw a policeman in a suit walking along the path behind the buildings she'd been hiding in. She opened her mouth to yell just as a large hand covered half her face and stifled her cry.

"I don't care what Zeus says," Apollo hissed in her ear. "I'm going to make you scream for mercy before I finish you off once and for all."

Zeus answered his phone, and this time just listened, looked down the road for a moment, then hung up and backed away from the fence.

"What's happening?" Rella asked, but her kidnapper just laughed and fumbled with his phone to bring up a GPS map.

Pushing the speed limit but trying not to rush too much and draw attention, Zeus took a series of roads, ending up on a divided highway. Suddenly, he braked and turned left into what appeared to Rella to be a thicket of shrubs. She closed her eyes, waiting for some kind of impact, but all she heard was the scraping of branches along the sides of the SUV. She hoped the car ended up scratched all to hell.

Opening her eyes, she saw a dirt lane that quickly turned into a narrow, paved road passing apartments on their right, before reaching warehouse buildings that looked familiar. Rella suddenly realized they'd looped around and come onto the road by the field from the other direction.

Zeus slowed and stopped by the opening in the tall fence

that surrounded the industrial park. Out the front window, Rella could see that the road kinked slightly, hiding them from the police car guarding the field.

From behind one of the buildings, Apollo appeared, dragging a beaten-looking Harper with him.

"Harper!" Rella called out, but with the windows up, no one could hear her.

Zeus laughed. "Your friend has caused us a bunch of trouble, but we're smarter than you think."

Harper suddenly wrenched herself free of Apollo's grip. She whipped around and landed a solid kick on his beefy thigh before turning and running. But Apollo was hardly fazed by her attack and caught her in a few steps, launching himself on top of her and bringing them both down on the grass. The last bit of energy knocked out of her, she struggled to move under his bulk.

Zeus jumped out of the SUV, stomped over to Harper, shoved Apollo off her, and yanked her up off the ground. He attempted to pin her arms behind her back, but she dropped her weight, throwing him off balance as she swung her elbow into his sternum then rotated her fist into his nose. She attempted to sweep his feet from under him, but he caught her leg and sent her flying to the ground, where she landed face down on the grass.

"Leave her alone," Rella yelled. She'd jumped out of the SUV, having scrambled across to the driver's door. "You've got me, and I'm the one with the money." She ran to them and grabbed Zeus's arm as he was about to hit Harper again.

He backhanded Rella across the face, hard enough that she flew back and hit the side of the SUV. She held her face and inched away. Zeus stomped back to where Apollo stood over Harper, each of them grabbing an arm and a leg and carrying her back to the car. Zeus dropped Harper's leg and opened the back door, and they pitched her inside, where she landed half on the seat and half on the floor. Zeus went after Rella, grabbed her arm before she could run, dragged her back to the SUV, and shoved her in the back. The two men moved to the front of the vehicle, squared off, and began yelling at one another.

"Are you okay?" Rella asked Harper as she helped her up onto the seat.

Harper groaned, sporting a new set of bruises to go with the rest. "I got away for a while, but I couldn't find the cops and he grabbed me again."

The two kidnappers abruptly stopped arguing and looked to the skies. Rella and Harper fell silent and listened for whatever had distracted the two men. The familiar whomp, whomp, whomp of helicopter blades crushing the air grew louder, and Apollo and Zeus lunged back inside the SUV, the latter slamming the vehicle in reverse and spinning the tires as they lurched backward down the road.

Where the mysterious man had disappeared to, they had no idea, so Nora and Whittaker had searched the warehouses, found no one to question, and returned to the scrubland via Courts Road. On the way, Nora had noticed the street kinked where the industrial park met the open scrubland, and with the last building obscuring their view, the constables watching the entrance couldn't see much beyond the warehouse. The pickup truck must have driven away from them unsighted.

Now, Whittaker used Nora's handheld radio to order the constables out of the woods and back to the field. They both knew too much time had passed, and with so much ground to cover, it was unlikely a proper sweep of the warehouses and the apartments would flush out the tall suspect, but perhaps they'd find the pickup. It would be nice to know exactly what the worker had witnessed.

Nora knew their own search around the warehouses had been easy to evade. All the suspect had to do was stay one building away and they'd never have seen him. It had struck her as weird he'd appeared alone, and she feared for what had happened to the woman who she was convinced he'd been with. Or had been chasing. *Perhaps she'd got away?*

Nora heard tires screeching in the distance just as the radio crackled to life and the helicopter copilot's smooth, calm voice didn't do the excitement of his news justice.

"Sierra One, this is X-Ray, Sierra One, this is X-Ray. We have a black SUV reversing at speed on Courts Road towards the bypass, over."

Nora sprinted toward the detective's SUV with Whittaker not far behind, breathing heavily as he simultaneously ran and tried to talk into the radio.

"X-Ray, this is Sierra One, X-Ray, this is Sierra One. Keep eyes on the vehicle, we'll be in pursuit."

Nora reached Whittaker's shiny silver Range Rover and paused, looking back. He hit the unlock, then tossed her the key fob.

"Don't kill us, or anyone else, Nora," he barked, and continued to the passenger side.

Nora suppressed a grin and jumped in the driver's seat, ready to put the key in the ignition. But there was no key on the fob, and no place to put one, just a button with the word "start" backlit and flashing at her. She hit the button and the engine smoothly purred to life. Unsure what to do with the fob, she dropped it into a cup holder, pulled the shifter into drive, and pushed the throttle down, expecting the powerful motor to light up the tires on the loose surface next to the road. Instead, the engine began to subtly hesitate, and the SUV pulled away without a slip of a wheel.

"Traction control," Whittaker said from the passenger seat, fighting to get his belt secured.

Nora saw an icon flashing on the dash, which went away once they were on the pavement and accelerating down Courts Road in the direction of what was supposed to be a dead end.

"That sucks," she mumbled, eyeing the dashboard for an obvious button to disable the safety function.

"Leave it on," Whittaker ordered, his voice slightly panicked. "Remember, the goal is not to kill us, or endanger the public!"

"Sierra One, this is X-Ray. They're heading east on the bypass," came the voice from the helicopter over the radio.

The detective keyed the mic. "Is there a gap in the central divider?" he asked, foregoing the radio formalities.

"No sir," came the reply. "They're moving counter traffic."

Whittaker reached over and switched on the flashing lights and the siren, which seemed to scream from everywhere around the Range Rover. He then crossed himself.

"Continue in pursuit," he told Nora with little conviction. "Try and use the hard shoulder unless the traffic has clearly pulled over."

In Nora's head she affirmed the order, but no words came out of her mouth. She was too focused on controlling the bouncing SUV on what had become a very bumpy dirt trail. The SUV burst through a narrow gap in the shrubs lining Esterly Tibbetts Highway, the divided highway which bypassed Seven Mile Beach and downtown George Town, where she skidded the big vehicle to the right, keeping tight to the edge of the road.

Several cars were moving away slowly, having stopped to let the madman in the black SUV race past them, going the wrong way. Seeing the police lights and blaring siren, they slammed on their brakes and stopped again, forming a chicane which Nora deftly weaved through, accelerating all the time.

"Careful, careful," Whittaker wheezed, clutching at the door handle.

"Sierra One, this is X-Ray. You're clear for three hundred meters before more slow-moving traffic."

Nora nodded and pushed the throttle pedal to the floor, the eight-cylinder engine smoothly racing the SUV up to 80 mph in a matter of seconds.

"That's enough, that's good," Whittaker urged, but Nora kept accelerating.

Up ahead, more traffic sped toward them at an alarming closing rate with the combined speeds, but each vehicle pulled to the side in self-preservation as the Range Rover shot by, topping 100 mph.

"Nora!" Whittaker growled, but she was already braking as they approached the big roundabout by the A.L. Thompson Hardware building and the exit toward the airport.

"Heads up for confused traffic in roundabout," the copilot called out, his silky voice beginning to speed up in tandem with the escalating action below the chopper. "Suspect took the short way to Godfrey Nixon Way."

Confused was one way of putting it, Nora decided. Chaotic would be more accurate. Still running against traffic, she wound her way between a mixture of stationary vehicles, people braking in panic, and a few rushing to get away from the melee. Once she'd maneuvered the Range Rover on to Godfrey Nixon, she could see the black SUV up ahead. The driver was finally using the left lane, but spent more time in the central turning lane, dodging in and out of traffic.

With a combination of flashing lights and the fact that commuters had just dodged the first errant vehicle, most people veered out of her path, and Nora began quickly catching the fleeing black SUV.

"Central, do we have anyone up ahead for a roadblock?" Whittaker shouted into the radio to be heard over the sirens.

"On which road, sir?" the dispatcher asked.

"We're heading east on… watch for that one!" Whittaker yelled, with the mic still keyed.

The fugitives swerved to the right-hand side of the road and slid through the intersection, ignoring the red light at Eastern Avenue. Nora followed, opening up the arc of the corner by hurtling over the center divider with a violent thump from the tires, finishing the corner in the left lane.

"We're now heading north on Eastern... uhh," the detective groaned as he was thrust forward into his seat belt as Nora braked as hard as the heavy vehicle would allow, the ABS brake system purring and the pedal vibrating under her foot.

She swung the Range Rover left, closing even more on the black SUV as she used the sidewalk as her apex, grabbing a few extra feet of room to keep her speed up. They were now only four car lengths behind and could see the vehicle was badged GMC Yukon and had four occupants being tossed around inside as the driver swerved left and right on the curving street.

"Bodden Road heading toward the water," Whittaker spluttered into the radio.

"Sierra One, expect traffic on North Church. Road is not clear. I repeat, road is not clear."

Bodden Road narrowed and curved around a building before meeting the two-lane waterfront street ahead. The black SUV's brake lights suddenly glowed brightly as they spotted the T-junction, and Nora braked at the same time, giving herself four car lengths more margin.

"Oh no!" Whittaker fumed as they watched the vehicle they were chasing swerve left through the intersection onto the busy street, unable to slow down enough.

The Yukon slid across the road, clipping the rear corner of a car heading north, spinning the helpless tourist like a top. The heavy SUV was knocked sideways and fishtailed several times, using the parking area in front of a waterfront business as room to recover, then dodged across oncoming traffic to the left lane and sped away.

Nora brought the Range Rover to a sliding stop before entering North Church and made sure no more cars were involved, before accelerating around the stopped traffic and resuming pursuit. She'd lost all her hard-earned gain on the Yukon, which was now several hundred yards ahead, ducking in and out of traffic, causing cars to take avoiding action all along their path.

Whittaker called in the incident over the radio, then clung to the door handle and the dashboard. "We don't need any more civilians involved, Nora. They can't go far on the island, and we have eyes on them from above."

Nora knew that was true, but she wasn't ready to give up the chase. Most of the traffic ahead on both sides were gladly pulling to the side for the police vehicle, happy they hadn't been hit by the lunatic in the Yukon. Nora sped back up to 80 mph, running straight down the middle of the road, straddling the solid white no passing line.

"Sierra One, suspect vehicle is stopping!" came the call from the helicopter, the copilot's voice now just as excited as Nora's pulse rate. "They've pulled over at the fish market and are exiting the vehicle."

Ahead, fifty yards before where the local fishermen sold their daily catch from a table under a small tent on a short stretch of sandy beach, a box truck tried turning inland on Mary Street, finding the gap between stopped cars too small, and blocking the road. Nora stood on the brakes, once again throwing her boss into the clutches of his seat belt.

"*Fy faen!*" Nora growled. "Call Ben, sir!"

Nora laid on the horn, but the traffic in front of her had gridlocked themselves and were making painstakingly small and slow shuffles to unclog the mayhem.

"Joint Marine Unit One, this is Sierra One, what's your twenty, over?" Whittaker urgently called over the radio.

After a long pause, Ben's voice replied. "Sierra One, this is Joint Marine Unit One. We're refueling in George Town harbor, sir."

"Joint Marine Unit One, this is Sierra One. We'll be with you in two minutes, be ready to pursue suspects on the water."

16

Apollo opened the back door and dragged Harper from the SUV, his gun in his other hand. His face glowed red with rage and his eyes darted around like a wild, cornered predator. If Harper hadn't believed the man would shoot her before, she was convinced now and allowed him to steer her down the steps onto the beach with a vise-like grip on her arm.

Behind her, Rella screamed, and Zeus swore at her, spittle flying from his mouth as he followed them toward the startled men at the little fish market. One of the fishermen held a large, very sharp knife that he'd been using to fillet a red snapper. Apollo aimed his gun at the man, who instantly dropped the knife to the sand.

"Whose boat?" Apollo demanded, waving his gun toward a faded blue wooden skiff pulled up to the sand.

The man who'd dropped the knife reluctantly raised his hand.

"Let's go. Now!" Apollo yelled, waving his gun at the fisherman.

The local trotted toward the boat, picking a small anchor

from the sand on the way and tossing it, along with the line, into the bow.

"You have to help, man," he said, pushing on the bow but looking back at the two thugs, each holding a pretty lady by the arm. "Tide gone out some, gotta push it."

Zeus turned to the other two fishermen. "Help him, damn it!"

The two men joined their friend while Apollo waded into the warm, clear water and heaved Harper into the smelly skiff. She landed with a thud and groaned. Every inch of her body ached, and her head was throbbing from the concussion she presumed he'd already given her.

Zeus followed suit with Rella; then the two men joined the locals in shoving the skiff free of the sand. Rella pushed herself to her knees, noting that the wailing siren hadn't come any closer since they'd skidded to a stop by the fish market.

"I thought we were all going to die in a fiery crash," she complained to Harper. "Are you okay?"

Harper rolled over and winced. Every part of her that touched anything felt cut or bruised. "Still kicking," she joked, although she doubted she could lift her leg high enough to kick anything above her ankle.

"They can't go far in this heap," Rella said, shifting to a seated position on the grubby, damp deck and looking up as a helicopter was flying straight toward them.

The rotor wash was whipping the surface of the water and blowing her hair in all directions, but she knew it could do little more than track them. There was nowhere to land a chopper, as far as she could see, and if the occupants were armed, surely they would have taken a shot at the kidnappers by now.

The skiff rocked about and slid backward until Rella felt the boat begin to float. Zeus shoved the fisherman alongside his own vessel and ordered him to get in. The man looked at the two women already aboard, his eyes full of sympathy, but with a gun to his back, there was little he could do beyond comply. Hopping over the side, he stepped to the battered-looking wooden helm station and started the outboard engine.

Zeus climbed into the boat, which sank into the sand once again, burdened by the extra weight. "Push more!" he screamed at Apollo and the other two fishermen. "We need to be deeper."

In the distance, the police siren from the silver SUV that had chased them was moving once more, and Rella looked at Harper with a glimmer of hope. "They're coming," she hissed.

"Shut the hell up!" Zeus demanded, the boat now floating once more. "Get in, get in!" he screamed at Apollo.

The big man lumbered through the water from the bow, but one of the fishermen reached out and grabbed his shirt, pulling him off balance and toppling him backward into the ocean. Both men leapt on top of Apollo and held him under until the deafening report of a gun went off next to Rella's ear.

One of the fishermen violently jolted, a burst of blood coming from the back of his shoulder as the bullet passed through his body. He splashed into the water, and the second fisherman immediately released Apollo and dived under the surface.

Rella screamed and bashed Zeus's arm aside as a second shot rang out. Apollo stumbled to his feet, coughing, spluttering, and swearing as he clambered alongside the skiff and swung himself over the side. Zeus slapped the side of Rella's head with his free hand, then swung around and pointed his gun at the fisherman behind him. The local gritted his teeth, knowing he'd been too slow to react when his friends had overpowered Apollo.

"Get us out of here, now!" Zeus ordered.

The fisherman dropped the transmission in reverse and

eased the skiff away from the sandy shore as Rella and Harper watched the third local man help his wounded friend back to the beach. The police siren echoed off the buildings, and they watched the silver Range Rover flash by the fish market without stopping.

"Where are they going?" Harper groaned. "We're right here."

"To get a bigger boat than this one," Zeus snarled, turning to the fisherman at the helm. "South to Sunset House. And you better take us as fast as this piece of shit will go or it'll be the last thing you do."

The man nodded and swung the skiff around to face south, but before he could open up the throttle, Apollo stepped to his side, grabbed him, and shoved him out of the boat. "I'm driving," he barked as the startled man splashed into the ocean.

Apollo pulled the throttle back, and the bow lifted into the air as the skiff shot forward.

"Move them up front!" he commanded, and Zeus waved his gun at the two women, who tried their best to scramble forward as the boat skipped and leapt across the water.

"This lump of driftwood goes faster than I'd hoped," Rella grumbled as she clawed her way to the bow.

"Typical," Harper added, flopping down beside her as the bow settled into the water. "Just our luck they steal the Ferrari of ancient fishing boats."

17

Nora ran down the concrete dock toward the *Cayman Defender*, the Royal Cayman Islands Joint Marine Unit's sixty-five-foot Dauntless RAM Patrol boat. Several officers were hurriedly removing the fueling hose and preparing to untie the lines. She leapt aboard and hurried into the wheelhouse where Ben was starting the twin MAN 1100-hp diesel engines.

"Chase the helicopter," Nora said. "They're staying above the fishing boat we're after."

"Yeah, I bin listening in," Ben replied without looking her way. "Clear da lines," he ordered into a mic which broadcasted across the boat's speakers.

"Whittaker," Nora muttered and turned to look out the rear windows of the cabin.

Detective Whittaker was out of breath, but an officer helped him onto the rear deck, then brought the stern line with him as he too stepped aboard. Nora looked beyond them to where the *DSTP* sat moored to the tender dock. On the swim step stood Captain Hall, watching the excitement transpire.

"*Drittsekk*," Nora mumbled to herself.

Ben eased into the throttles and pulled the boat away from

the dock, wasting little time increasing the power so the bow rose and a deep guttural throb emanated from the engine room. He flicked a switch and powerful red and blue lights reflected off the deck from the LEDs on the roof.

Whittaker opened the rear door and hauled himself inside. "I thought you were going to leave me behind, Ben," he managed between gasps.

Ben laughed. "Nora here said to go ahead without you, but I overruled her."

Nora shook her head but was too focused on their prey to debate the point. Beyond the harbor, the police chopper had its nose dipped so the pilot and copilot could watch the occupants as they tracked them from two hundred yards above and one hundred yards behind the skiff. Once clear of Hog Sty Bay harbor, Ben opened up the throttles and brought the patrol boat up on plane, quickly reaching thirty knots.

"You're armed, right?" Nora asked.

"Always," Ben replied, his eyes on the helicopter, then scanning side to side every few seconds, making sure the waters ahead were clear of boat traffic.

"We can't risk the hostages," Whittaker pointed out. "We'd need a clear shot."

"What is that?" Nora blurted, staring down the southwestern coastline.

"Looks like a seaplane," Whittaker said, seeing the object bobbing in the water more than half a mile away.

"Been there three or four days," Ben commented. "No idea who it belongs to."

"These guys, I'm guessing," Nora speculated. "Can we call air traffic control?"

"And say what?" Whittaker replied.

"Don't give them permission to take off. They control seaplanes the same as regular air traffic, right?"

"What makes you think they'll be asking for permission?" Whittaker scoffed.

"Won't matter," Ben interjected. "I'll catch dem before dey reach the seaplane. You best get ready for a hostage negotiation."

The *Cayman Defender* had eased up to its top speed of thirty knots, slicing through the calm water with ease. Ahead, the skiff was bouncing and skittering about, managing twenty-five knots at best. Nora realized Ben was right, they'd be upon the blue fishing boat shortly before it reached the seaplane. They were close enough to make out the two women near the bow and the larger of the kidnappers at the helm.

Whittaker spoke into the radio, "X-Ray, this is Sierra One, can you get low enough to divert them? Over."

"Sierra One, this is X-Ray. We'll give it a go. Over."

Nora watched the police helicopter sprint ahead of the skiff and drop swiftly until they were only what appeared to be a few feet off the water.

"I don't think this is a great idea, sir," she urged.

The second henchman raised his arm and fired at the chopper.

"Abort, abort!" Whittaker yelled into the radio, but the pilot wasn't waiting on an order, he'd already pulled back on the collective and opened the throttle, lifting the chopper clear of the water and out of harm's way.

"Sorry guys," Whittaker said over the radio.

"That's okay, sir. Doubt he'd hit us with a handgun from a boat, but I'd hate to be us if he had a lucky day."

"As you were, X-Ray," Whittaker added. "Appreciate the effort."

The patrol boat was now bearing down on the skiff, with only a few hundred yards until they reached the seaplane.

"We've got another problem, sir," Nora said, pointing to a

dive boat moored to a dive buoy halfway to the seaplane, off to the port side.

"They're out of our path," Ben assured her.

"They won't be when these *drittsekker* figure out we're going to catch them."

No sooner had she finished saying the words, the smaller villain pointed to the dive boat and yelled at his cohort. The skiff veered to port, heading straight for the dive boat.

"I don't like this," Whittaker muttered.

Nora recognized the dive boat. It belonged to friends of AJ's—Chris and Kate Alpers, who ran Indigo Divers—the name painted down the side of their large twin-outboard center console. Divers had just returned to the boat, and it looked like Kate was seated on the transom, getting ready to drop her BCD and tank. Everyone on the dive boat turned and looked as an errant fishing boat charged toward them with a helicopter overhead and the *Cayman Defender* in hot pursuit.

The skiff didn't slow but turned just in time to sweep by the stern of Indigo Divers and the smaller thug raised his gun one more time and fired at the helpless onlookers. With the noise of the diesels and the thick glass of the pilothouse, Nora couldn't hear the shots, but she watched in horror as the handgun recoiled several times in the man's hand.

The divers all ducked and covered their heads, but sitting on the transom, Kate was violently spun around and tumbled over the back into the water.

"We have to stop, Ben," Whittaker ordered, and Nora bolted out the side door, running to the port side.

The water behind the center console erupted in a fountain of spray, even reaching Nora as Ben put the big patrol boat's transmission in reverse and dragged it to a stop.

"Kate!" her husband screamed, running to the stern.

The churned up water began to settle, and Kate's BCD

broke the surface first. Her aluminum tank was split apart, which explained the eruption from the compressed air violently escaping.

Dazed, surprised, but unhurt, Kate picked her head up out of the water and took a deep breath.

"Is everyone okay?" Nora yelled.

"Define okay," Kate shouted back. "I'm not hurt, but was shot at and had my scuba tank explode, so I wouldn't say I'm in a great mood!"

Chris shook his head. "You scared the shit out of me."

"So, everyone on the boat is okay, Chris?" Nora hurriedly asked again.

"Yeah, yeah," he replied, making another quick check with his three customers. "We're fine."

Nora turned and frantically waved at Ben to continue the pursuit. Whittaker, who'd stayed in the wheelhouse calling in emergency services, now stuck his head out the door.

"Are you sure there's no one who needs medical attention?"

"I'm sure," Nora bellowed. "Let's go!"

Ben opened up the throttles and the patrol boat roared into life once more, now with only a hundred meters to cover until they reached the seaplane. He ordered two armed men to the bow and, over the speakers, told Nora to return to the pilot-house. She ignored the call and stayed at the railing, watching the propeller begin to turn on the seaplane. She slapped the rail with her hand.

"*Faen ta deg!*" she growled at the plane, watching the skiff float away and the plane's door close.

The line from the seaplane to the mooring had already been cut and as Ben raced to maneuver the Cayman Defender into the path of the seaplane, his two armed officers waited for orders. The propeller spun faster, and the engine growled above the sound of the patrol boat as the pilot tried to outrun them before their takeoff lane was blocked.

"Engine!" Ben barked over the speakers. "Aim for the engine!"

But as Ben swung the patrol boat around the side of the seaplane, the pilot was already running as fast as the boat and used the tail rudder to rotate away from his pursuer. The marksmen couldn't get a clean shot from the bouncing boat without risking hitting anyone in the cockpit, and after a few more moments, all they could do was slow to a stop and watch the seaplane lift from the water and fly away from their jurisdiction.

Whittaker joined Nora at the bow. "I called the airport. they're busy screaming at them over the radio, which I doubt will do any good, but they'll report the tail number to all the airports within range."

"We don't have a plane we can send after them?" Nora asked.

Whittaker shook his head. "Unless you've noticed a Cayman Islands Air Force tucked away somewhere I don't know about, then no, we don't have any planes. Besides, what could another plane do apart from follow them?"

Nora slapped the railing again and swore under her breath. "So, what now?"

"Now," he replied, rubbing his forehead. "You and I will be filling out reports and paperwork 'til Christmas."

Nora groaned. She hated paperwork nearly as much as she hated watching the kidnappers get away with Cabot and Finn. "Wait," she blurted. "Before we do that shit, we need to interview Captain Hall."

"If we can find him," Whittaker countered.

"That's easy," she grinned. "He's back on the *DSTP*. He watched us chase his buddies away."

18

Rella pressed her cheek to the window and watched the police patrol boat get smaller behind them as Zeus kept the seaplane dangerously close to the water. Harper was slumped, exhausted, in the seat across the narrow aisle. Behind them, instead of more seats, was a cargo area half-full of large tanks of some sort.

For the first hour, no one spoke. Rella and Harper both knew that whatever ideas of escape they'd been conjuring in their minds had now vanished… or at least reset with a fresh set of challenges. On the positive side, they weren't dead, Rella thought, so their kidnappers still planned to get her money, which might lead to another opportunity.

They passed near several populated land masses, though neither could name the countries. Rella tried to picture a Caribbean map in her mind but soon gave up, as she wasn't even sure in which direction they were flying.

Reading their minds, Zeus told them, "We're flying around the eastern tip of Cuba in order to stay out of their airspace."

Hours passed, or so it seemed, and finally, Zeus landed on

the water. He cruised up to a dock and parked in front of a fuel tank.

Rella leaned forward. "We need to use the bathroom, and you need to feed us." They'd already learned that there wasn't a bathroom on board.

Apollo was ready to fight them, but Harper cut him off. "If you don't let us at least use the bathroom, I'll go on the seat and do worse on the floor." At his look of horror, she yelled, "And water," adding "a-holes" under her breath.

"Take them both," Zeus grumbled.

"Step out of line, and you know what will happen." Apollo jerked Harper to her feet and pushed her over to the exit.

Rella followed to avoid being roughed up.

On the dock, a small sign identified the area as Walters Cay, the northern tip of the Bahamas. Apollo pointed to a wooden shack, clearly an outhouse. "You were complaining about needing a bathroom." It sat next to another run-down building that served food to go. One man sat on the pier eating his order.

Apollo waited outside the door until the two women came back out.

"That was damn disgusting," Harper sneered at Apollo, who shrugged: *Tough.*

He stepped over to the neighboring shack and picked up several bags waiting for him. Once they were all back on the plane and seated, he threw the bags at the women. At least he'd sprung for some water.

They took off, flying for hours before landing again, this time on land.

"Now where are we?" Harper yelled. Neither man acknowledged her.

Zeus taxied the plane over to a tiny terminal.

"Do they have an outhouse here?" Harper yelled. "How about some more awful food?"

Rella looked out the window and guessed they were back in the States, as the building didn't resemble anything they'd seen in the islands.

Zeus nodded to Apollo, who wasn't happy being saddled with the women once again. He opened the door. "Pretty sure you remember the rules," he warned as they went by him and down the ladder. "The can is on the side of the building."

"We're somewhere on the Eastern Shore of Virginia." Rella pointed to a sign that read, "Accomack County Airport, The Heart of Virginia's Eastern Shore."

Harper tugged her into the unisex bathroom and ensured the door was locked. "At least it doesn't smell as bad as the last one. Thought I'd be sick."

Rella nodded. "How long do you think we can stay in here before he kicks the door down?"

They found out minutes later when Apollo started to beat on the door. "There's a line out here," he shouted.

"Hold your water," Harper shouted back. "Too bad the window's not accessible." She stared at the window over the door. "If it were even reachable, we'd land on Apollo's head, maybe break his neck. How satisfying would that be?" She grinned.

Rella opened the door and scanned the walkway; there were no other people in sight.

Apollo glared at the two of them. "Took you long enough."

"Where's the line?" Harper groused. "One look at your inviting smile, and they ran off?"

"Once we get to where we're going, I'll get you something to eat. Don't bother telling me what you want; I'm not taking food orders." He pointed to the plane like they didn't know the way.

"When you do, how about picking up another pair of cheap shoes for Harper? I'm happy to reimburse you the dollar." Rella looked down at her friend's bruised feet and winced. She didn't know how she was still getting around.

"You're in our playground now, and shooting you wouldn't have anyone looking twice. They're too busy minding their own business or doing a little shooting of their own. Around here, they get rid of bodies and make sure they never resurface."

"Try getting money out of a corpse." *So there* was inferred on Rella's face.

Harper hooked her arm through Rella's. "Hang onto your sanity until we get to wherever we're going."

The two climbed back in the plane, and Apollo closed the door with a bang.

Zeus turned in his seat. "You two should be nicer to Apollo. He's shown a lot of patience where you're concerned. The bruises you two are sporting are your own fault."

"How much farther until we get to wherever?" Harper asked in a civilized tone.

"Not far. We're going to a private cabin on the coastal Virginia inside passage. You'll find your accommodations there better than the last."

"When is the money transfer happening so you can be rid of the two of us?" Rella asked.

"Good question," Zeus mumbled, turned his back on them, and got on his phone.

"Do you think his spirited conversation has anything to do with us?" Harper chuckled humorlessly.

"When he gets that edge to his tone, he's talking to whoever the head honcho is. We already know it isn't him." Rella checked to make sure Zeus wasn't listening to them.

Zeus was right when he said they weren't far from their

destination. They once again landed on the water, this time in front of a smallish house on stilts. It was at the far end of an island that faced a small bay located on a shallow inlet. There wasn't another thing in sight. They pulled up to a rickety dock in front of the house.

Apollo had the door open as soon as they stopped and was up the steps to the front door, and not once had he checked to see if the women were following. He was back in a flash, standing in front of them on the dock. "I left the door unlocked."

"You're leaving us here?" Rella shouted as he started up the ladder of the seaplane.

Apollo turned and said, "You want food, right? Well, Door-Dash doesn't deliver out here. So get up into the house and stay there until we get back. And before you think about trying to run off, there's nowhere to go. Just miles of deserted beach, if you can even make it that far through the marsh and the snakes. Schools of sharks in the inlet, too. Just chill out until we get back with the food and set up the satellite internet. And you're gonna want to be inside before the mosquitoes and biting flies figure out you're here." He climbed up into the plane.

"You don't need to rush getting back," Harper yelled as he closed the door. She and Rella stood there as the plane took off. "Now what?"

19

Casey and Dawn Shaw pulled up in front of the large thatched chickee hut that served as an open-air restaurant and bar at the Bluffs Marina during the warmer months of the year. The couple were the main partners in a group that owned the property and several other waterfront businesses in Virginia.

As they walked through the chickee, several male heads turned toward Dawn—a stunning woman with long red hair and blue eyes, in her early thirties and only an inch shy of her six-foot husband. She led the way through the building and out onto the patio deck, which overlooked the marina. The couple then wove their way through a sea of tables to the edge of the deck, where two of their good friends sat waiting. Both of these women were also shareholders in the Shaws' property group.

Rikki Jenkins was the owner of a national private security firm based on the Eastern Shore of Virginia. In her early thirties, she was tall and very toned, with short-cropped, naturally platinum-blond hair and stunning ice-blue eyes. The other woman was her partner, Cindy Crenshaw, the executive vice president of the Shaws' property management group. She was an inch or two shorter, very shapely with below-the-shoulder curly blond hair and bluish-gray eyes. While Cindy was a few years older than Rikki, it wasn't easy to tell. The two lived aboard their older fifty-two-foot Hatteras motor yacht at the Bayside Resort, about ten minutes away.

Dawn noted the half-empty glasses in front of their friends as she and Casey sat down. "Glad you didn't let us hold you up."

"Good wine never waits on anyone." Rikki grinned.

Cindy said, "We got here early. This view is always great, but it's even better with wine." She held her glass up in a mock toast toward the marina, about twenty feet below the bluff where the deck was located.

"Are you ready for tomorrow, Rik?" Casey asked.

"Always ready to go fly fishing, pal. Especially for tarpon."

The area was the farthest north where tarpon could be found. Though not as prevalent here in Virginia as they are in the Florida Keys, this higher degree of difficulty in finding them was what made catching and releasing one so satisfying. Known as "Silver Kings," they were one of the more acrobatic fish species. And the fight of a large "poon" can be enough to exhaust even the most proficient fly-fisherman.

Casey said, "Good. We'll meet here at about seven thirty. There's no sense in getting to Metompkin Inlet before the sun is high enough to spot the bubbles or see fish rolling."

During the fishing season, Casey kept his flats boat on a lift here at the Bluffs. Their run to Metompkin would take a little less than twenty minutes.

Tarpon are a unique product of evolution. Over the millennia, they have developed a swim bladder that also acts as a kind of lung, allowing them to breathe in water with a low oxygen count and when they are out of the water altogether. They can take in gulps of air when they roll on the surface, leaving a bubble trail as they slowly exhale underwater. This bladder is also one of the reasons that they're such great fighters, being able to take in more oxygen during their leaps.

Rikki nodded. "Sounds like a plan."

Suddenly Casey's attention was diverted toward Burton's Bay as an airplane came into view. The pilot was throttling back, and the change in sound was what first grabbed his attention. The second thing was that it was equipped with pontoons for landing on water.

Now the other three turned to see what Casey was watching. The blue-and-white plane slowly turned into the wind just beyond the marsh's edge. They watched as it made a perfect landing, slowing as the pontoons settled into the water just a few yards short of the Bluffs channel. It turned into the narrow but deep cut that led into the marina.

When Casey had laid out the plan for building the docks, he had included a small floating dock specifically designed for tying up a seaplane. Sam Knight, the chief pilot of Shaw Air—Casey and Dawn's aircraft charter company—had been trying to talk them into buying a seaplane for their operation. Sam came to the operation licensed to fly small jets, multi-engine prop planes, and seaplanes. The latter was something he kept reminding Casey about, especially since Casey also liked flying prop planes, though he hadn't yet been rated for seaplanes.

"Uh-oh, you're in for it now, Case." Dawn pointed at a man emerging from an A-frame house set on pilings at the base of the first dock. He looked to be in his mid-forties and was a dead ringer for a young Sam Elliott, the actor. Sam Knight had spotted the plane and was hurrying over to the seaplane dock.

Casey grimaced, knowing that this encounter would give Sam another dose of "seaplane envy." It didn't help matters that the arriving plane was the exact model he'd been pitching to Casey, a turboprop Cessna 208 Grand Caravan EX Amphibian.

Sam hurried out to the small floating dock as the plane approached. He motioned that he would be happy to help with the dock lines, but the pilot waved him off from inside the cockpit. Still not one to give up a chance to chat with another seaplane pilot, Sam stayed out on the dock. The rear cabin door opened, and a burly-looking character emerged. He also waved Sam away as he attached his first line to a cleat on the rear of the pontoon.

The man then leaped across the short gap between the pontoon and the dock, securing the loose end to a dock cleat and arresting the plane's forward motion. The pilot "feathered" the propeller, meaning that he caused the blades to turn until they lost their pitch and were no longer angled to pull air past them. Flattening the pitch helped stop the prop's rotation after he shut down the engine. The passenger now repeated his same procedure with another dock line on the forward part of the pontoon, snugging the plane against the side of the dock.

The four friends on the deck watched as the pilot got out and stepped onto the dock, ignoring Sam's outstretched hand and words of welcome. Because this was happening over thirty yards away, they couldn't hear exactly what was said, though they could see from the pilot's body language that he wanted Sam to stay away from his aircraft. His passenger joined his side and shoved Sam over toward the main dock.

Seeing the altercation becoming physical, Casey jumped up and ran down the stairs that led to the docks. He reached Sam's side a few seconds later, just as the trio's voices increased in volume.

"Hey! Is there a problem here?" Casey asked rather forcefully.

The passenger pointed at him and said, "You need to mind your own business."

Sam said, "He is. That's my boss, and he owns this place."

Casey repeated, "Like I said, is there a problem here?"

The other man, the pilot, replied, "Yeah. I don't want anyone around my airplane or sticking their nose into my business. Your man here doesn't know how to take a hint and get lost when he's told to."

"Well, 'my man' is my pilot and friend who also happens to live here and keeps an eye on things for me. If you give him any more trouble, you'll be the ones getting lost."

The man now held up his hands in protest. "Look, we just came here to get some food and not get hassled. But I don't want anybody messing with my plane while we eat."

Casey replied, "We'll make sure that nobody goes near your plane. So why don't you go on up and eat, and then you can get back out of here before it gets dark."

With a sideways glance toward his partner, the pilot nodded then the two started toward the stairs. When they reached the base, the passenger turned and glared at Casey and Sam, who were still standing in the same spot and watching the two as they left.

Now out of earshot, Casey commented to Sam, "Nice guys."

"Grade A number one jerks. Over the years, I've met a few like them around airports, but thankfully, not many. These two are now at the top of that list. I was only being friendly, offering to help them tie up, but you'd have thought I'd kicked their dog instead. What I'd hoped would be an opportunity to talk to the pilot about his plane almost turned into a fistfight. They sure don't want anyone getting a close look at it."

Casey frowned. "That's strange."

"Yeah, not half as strange as what's in it. Before the guy

closed that back door, I saw it had what looked like a huge extra fuel tank in the back, definitely not standard equipment, and they'd taken out all but four of the seats. That model normally seats eight, including the pilot. I don't know if you noticed, but it's a Cessna Grand Cara…"

Casey interrupted him. "Yeah, I know what it is. But my question is, what do you think they're doing with it? With that much extra weight in fuel, it won't have that great a payload capacity. Carrying only three passengers certainly won't pay much."

"Well, all that fuel equals a much longer range, maybe a little more than fifty percent more. You'd have to carry a lot more ganja than it would hold to pay for that plane. But there's still quite a lucrative market for running cocaine and opioids. They aren't as bulky and bring big dollars. Anyway, that's my guess."

"All the more reason for them to eat up and get the hell out of here and for us to hope that they never come back. Even if they aren't smugglers, we don't need customers that look for reasons to cause trouble." Casey said.

"Yeah. So, on another subject, what do you think of the plane?" Sam asked hopefully.

"I think you're like a dog with a bone. Once you sink your teeth in one, you'll never let go."

Sam grinned. "Pretty slick, isn't it?"

Casey nodded, conceding the point. "We'll see how the year turns out, profit-wise. It might be a good tool for getting around to all our waterfront properties in the mid-Atlantic."

The two split up at the stairs, with Casey rejoining the three women and Sam returning to his house.

Dawn asked, "Crisis averted?"

Casey looked around for the two men before answering.

They weren't in sight, so he figured they were either in the chickee or the enclosed part of the restaurant.

"Yeah, for now. But there's something sketchy about those two." He lowered his voice so only the three could hear as he related what Sam told him and what he'd seen.

Rikki said, "I'll run their tail number when we get back to the boat. See if anything pops up."

Forty minutes later, they were finishing their dinner when the two men emerged from the chickee. They watched the pair as they loaded up in the Cessna and backed away from the dock. One of the neat features of turboprop planes is their ability to reverse the pitch of their propellers and go into reverse. Then the pilot spun his airplane around and taxied out the cut.

Once he reached Burton's Bay, the pilot pointed its nose into the wind and went to full throttle. The plane quickly got "on step" as the pontoons rose out of the water and began skimming across the surface. A few hundred yards later, it broke free and began gaining altitude. Casey noted that it only climbed to about 500 feet before leveling off and heading south.

Dawn said, "Good riddance."

"I hope that's the last we see of them," Casey said.

Cindy said, "It probably will be since we've never seen them nor their plane around before. I wouldn't worry about it."

Casey hoped that was true, but he had a nagging feeling still worrying him. He made a mental note to ask around the airport about them. If they were indeed up to something, he wanted to know about it.

20

After taking a look around the immediate vicinity, Rella and Harper stood on the beach with the ocean gently washing back and forth before them.

"The only thing that makes any sense as to why we were dumped here..." Rella began before pausing, glancing over her shoulder at the house on stilts, lost in thought. "At least it's better digs than the last couple of places," she finished.

"You were saying before you sidetracked yourself?" Harper responded, kicking water on her.

"It's cold!" Rella yelped, jumping back. "I was just thinking that someone must be looking for us, so that's why we were dropped off here. Our husbands know something has happened to the two of us, as they haven't heard from us. In addition, they haven't been able to get in touch, and they'd be all over it. Thinking that's why we were brought to the States; good luck tracking us here."

"We're going to get out of here." Harper scanned the beach and looked at the sunset.

"I'm so disoriented when it comes to time. No clue how long that plane ride took. You'd think they'd want their money and would be back, but when? The longer they drag their feet, one would think that they'd be worried about going to a bank. But then they know all I need is a laptop. Though doing it that way might garner red flags," Rella mused. "Since this isn't over with already, it has to be that something went wrong that we don't know about, and since they never tell us anything…"

"We're not going to sit around and wait to find out. Tomorrow we're going for a walk. Even though it doesn't look like it, something must be out there. If we see an inhabited island, then we go for a swim." Harper linked her arm around Rella's, and they trekked down the sand.

The only set of stairs was at the far end of the red-and-white house. The front door opened into a large living/dining room area. The room was devoid of anything except for a worn leather couch and two oversized chairs.

"This is cozy," Harper snarked.

"It's also dirty, which we should be getting used to after the last couple of places." Rella said, standing in the doorway while Harper went down the hallway to check out the rest of the rooms, which took about a minute.

"All the rooms are empty, clearly not expecting guests. We can fight over who gets the couch."

"From the outside, it didn't have that lived-in feel, but thought if I didn't say it, it wouldn't be so." Rella reached out and hit the light switch. "At least there's electricity." She followed Harper to the kitchen. "Please tell me there's food."

Harper opened all the cupboards and the refrigerator. "There's an array of no-named canned food, and as for the fridge, I'd take a pass as a couple of items have been in there long enough to discolor." At the sink, she turned on the taps. "At least the water's not dirty."

"What you're telling me is that canned food and tap water

are on the menu for dinner tonight and every other meal?" Rella covered her face and laughed.

"What do you suppose Zeus and Apollo use this house for? And why an empty house in a deserted place?"

"It's called a stash house for kidnap victims."

"Who knew a CEO rolled her eyes." Harper laughed.

Rella ignored her friend. "Having a few pieces of real estate in my portfolio, I'd think that unloading this property wouldn't be easy unless it was a fire sale, and even then."

Harper continued to open more cupboards, pulled a pot from one of them, and waved it. "I'm going to whip up some soup."

"I'm going to take the one-minute tour and be back to help you. I'll set the counter." Rella strode down the hallway, and all the rooms were empty; even though she knew Harper wasn't kidding, she hoped she was. Back in the kitchen, she poked through the cupboards and didn't find a single dish, but there were a couple of oversized mugs, so she took them out and set them on the counter. "Knowing your mind is a busy place, what have you planned to get us out of here? I should be more specific—back to civilization."

"After more soup for breakfast, we'll investigate this island and figure out where we are exactly if that's possible, and if there's anyone else around."

Once their one-course meal had been poured, they took it into the living room and sat on the couch instead of standing.

"Despite the isolation, this could be a cute place with a little work, and there's no discounting the gorgeous view from every room." Surrounded by water, Harper pointed to the beach in the near distance. "I'm assuming that's the Atlantic Ocean." She stuck out her leg and waved it. "Pretty sure I didn't tell you that once Grey laughed about putting a tracker in my ankle, mostly amusing himself. Now I wish he'd insisted."

"I'm sorry I didn't think more about our safety," Rella lamented.

Harper snorted. "Who'd have thought we'd get kidnapped off a luxury yacht—no one."

Once they finished the soup, Rella collected the mugs, took them back to the kitchen, rinsed them out, and went back to the living room.

Harper had pushed the chairs up next to the couch, arranging them so that there was plenty of room for the two to stretch out.

"This was clever of you." Rella nodded.

"No lying down just yet. You're not going to believe what I found, and it will save us from boredom." Harper took out a pack of Bicycle playing cards from her pocket, the well-worn box held together with tape.

They sat cross-legged, facing one another, and played until the room was dark, neither one getting up to turn on the light over the front door.

"Got to thinking that there's more than our husbands missing us, as we have businesses, meetings missed, and there's never been a time that we haven't shown up or not called."

"Add the yacht's owner, Decker, to that list, as you'd think he'd have sounded an alarm the night we disappeared. This wasn't a question I thought to ask, but have to wonder if there were cameras on board the yacht or the dock. If so, someone might be able to ID the men that took us." At least, Rella hoped.

"When our husbands invade the Caymans, and I'd be shocked if they weren't already there, they'll put pressure on anyone they think might have an answer. Neither are stupid, so there won't be any putting anything over on them."

"Maybe that's an answer as to why we were dumped here. Let's hope that if our disappearance heats up that Zeus and Apollo don't show back up here. If they've figured out there are eyes on them, they wouldn't want to do anything that would create attention."

The two talked until they fell asleep. The next morning, they both woke up to the sunlight streaming through the living room windows.

"How did you sleep?" Harper asked.

"Fitfully. I'd wake up and then try to talk myself into going back to sleep." Rella sat up. "I'm going to cook us breakfast."

The two laughed.

After finishing off their mugs of soup, the two hit the beach. Harper had found two empty water bottles on the floor of the pantry closet and rinsed them out, filling them with water from the tap.

They stood on the sand and decided to stay on the strip that ran along the water on the inner coastal side. To get to the Atlantic side, they'd have to cross a marshy area with an over-growth of greenery that appeared to have its roots in water.

"One good thing about this walk is we don't have to wear shoes and can save them for something special."

Rella laughed at Harper. But she did copy her when she shoved them inside her dress, the toes sticking out of her dress — one less thing to carry.

On their way to the island's far end, they passed several land masses off the Atlantic side. A couple were minuscule and appeared somewhat underwater. Once at the end of the sandy strip, they spotted an inhabited island off in the distance. Their option was to swim to the closest island and hope it was solid ground that they could walk across.

"I know you're trying to figure out how to get over to that distant island with the multitude of buildings, but it's not happening since swimming around might be our only option and thinking it could turn into a dangerous trek that we might not survive." Rella nudged Harper as the frustration oozed out of her.

"Hate to agree with you on this one."

"That's why they dumped us, knowing that the only way off this island is a boat or plane." Rella dropped to the sand and put her head on her knees.

Harper slid next to Rella. "We're going to figure out something."

"Your optimism is what will keep us going." Rella hugged her.

21

Once again, Rikki had beaten Casey to the Bluffs. He found her out at a table on the deck, finishing a cup of coffee. "Ready to go, Rik?"

"All set. I had them make us a couple of box lunches, and I've got water and sodas in the cooler."

She stood and picked up a bag with their lunch and her fishing gear while Casey grabbed the cooler and added it to the fishing gear he was carrying. Once out on the dock, he put the drain plug in the skiff and began lowering it into the water.

"I looked up that Cessna's registration, Case. It belongs to some LLC in Miami. That's all I could get on it because the tail number is blocked, so I couldn't track it or see any past flights."

Casey nodded. "Figures the tail number would be blocked. Seems like more are than aren't these days. Nobody wants to be tracked, and there are dozens of free tracking apps. But by flying as low as they were when they took off, they had to have been under visual flight rules anyway without a flight plan having been filed."

Rikki nodded in agreement. "Those two still felt sketchy."

Once the skiff was floating, they climbed aboard and were idling out through the cut less than a minute later. Casey opened the throttle as they sped across Burton's Bay and around the low-lying marsh islands between it and Big Wye Channel, then finally out through Wachapreague Inlet and into the Atlantic Ocean.

The sea was almost flat-calm, so Casey didn't need to slow down as he made their turn to the north. They ran along the coast of Cedar Island up to Metompkin Inlet, staying far enough offshore to avoid the stubs of submerged pilings that once supported dozens of oceanfront houses there.

At one point back in the 1950s, Cedar Island had been subdivided and platted into two thousand lots in some developer's grand vision of an oceanside utopia. But big problems emerged. A planned bridge from the mainland was never built, and the island—which was basically just a sandbar that bordered a marsh—was disappearing at the rate of up to thirteen feet per year.

The ocean and some powerful coastal storms slowly claimed the dozens of stilt houses that were built, and only a few of their owners removed the debris and the pilings after they collapsed. The only structure that remained standing on Cedar Island was the decommissioned Coast Guard station on the marsh side, far from the ocean's onslaught. Casey and Rikki saw it in the distance as they passed by.

A few minutes later, Casey turned into the inlet at the southern end of Metompkin Island. The island was now owned by the Virginia Barrier Island Conservation Foundation, a nonprofit group that was dedicated to stopping any future development by purchasing as much of the seaside land as possible. Buying Metompkin Island was one of VBICF's greatest accomplishments, as its beach was the prime nesting ground for one of the largest groups of endangered piping plovers and several species of sea turtles.

Fortunately, only one house was ever built on Metompkin, on the shore of a small bay just inside a hook-shaped sandbar bordering the southern inlet. But this house, too, was in danger of eventually being lost to the elements. The sand barrier that had protected it for so many years was also slowly eroding. But until the inevitable happened, it would continue to be used for rustic getaways by the larger benefactors of the VBICF. Their ability to reserve time at the house was one of the perks that came with those larger donations, in addition to the hefty tax write-offs.

A quick scan of the empty dock led Casey to believe the house was currently vacant. This made him happy since the little bay was their prime fishing spot for tarpon. More than once, they'd had to bypass it and move to another location when there were kids running around outside the house. Out on the dock, their presence scared the tarpon, which were notoriously skittish. Plus, you never want to let anyone in on your best spot. And unless any of those visitors knew what to look for, the tarpon there would remain a secret.

Rikki climbed up onto the casting platform on the bow as Casey idled slowly into the bay and then shut the outboard engine off. Rikki lowered the Rhodan GPS Trolling Motor into the water, which Casey then controlled from the stern with a wireless fob. It would allow them to cruise slowly and stealthily as they searched for their quarry. One touch of a button on the fob could hold the boat in the same location, regardless of the current or the wind, aided by the GPS receiver. It could also take them on the exact same course that he had stored from another trip to this same bay. Casey could also steer and control their speed with the fob as they fought fish.

Neither of them said a word as they concentrated on the surface of the water, watching for rolling tarpon. As they slowly made their way around the bay, Rikki spotted several tarpon rolling next to a mud flat. She glanced back and saw Casey nod, silently acknowledging that he, too, had seen them. They'd spent so much time fishing together that they could communicate without much need for speech. He steered the boat over toward what now appeared to be a school of several fish.

Rikki was watching the telltale wake of one of the fish on the edge of the school as she double-hauled her fly line, sending it back and forth in the air while adding more length to it with every pass. Finally, she sent the chartreuse-colored fly to a perfect landing a few feet in front of the fish. She began "stripping" the line back in by hand, unconsciously holding her breath while she did so.

Casey saw her hand hesitate, and then she raised the tip of her Sage carbon fiber rod as the water around the fish exploded. She let the retrieved fly line that had coiled at her feet play out between her fingers, adding slight friction to it until it was depleted. Then the line began screaming off her reel.

The giant fish—which Casey estimated somewhere around a hundred pounds—broke free of the water, twisting and turning wildly in midair. Rikki had become an expert at fighting tarpon and reacted instantly. She bent forward in a bow as she extended her rod arm. This gave the fish just enough slack to be able to complete its aerial acrobatics without breaking the monofilament tippet, but still not enough to allow it to dislodge the hook from its concrete-hard jaw. This defensive move is known as "bowing to the king" in reference to their nickname.

Once back underwater, the fish was running again, and

Rikki's fly reel was screaming against its drag. Casey sped up, the trolling motor now fighting to keep pace with the fish, which was headed out into the deeper water of the inlet. The fight continued another half an hour before Rikki could start gaining line back onto the reel. The leaps were now fewer and less spectacular, though still heart-stopping. During one of those final leaps, Casey noticed that same Cessna seaplane from last night in the distance, apparently lining up for a landing very near their position.

"Rik, we may have company. I think it's that same plane from last night."

"Yeah, Case, I see them. But they can't land on us."

"Let's hope they understand that, too."

But the plane didn't alter its direction. Casey realized that on its present course, it would either collide with them or pass way too close.

"What the hell is that idiot doing?" Casey began waving his arms franticly, trying to get the pilot's attention, seemingly without any result. The plane was now several hundred yards away, its pontoons starting to come in contact with the water as it began skipping across the surface. When it finally came down "off-step," with the pontoons settling into the water, its right wingtip passed by barely fifty feet away from their skiff. The rudder on the right pontoon hit Rikki's fly line, parting it and causing her to lose her fish.

Rikki shook her fist and yelled, "You stupid jerk!"

Neither man in the cockpit could hear her words over the whine of the turboprop engine, and they ignored her gestures completely.

"He saw our boat and could see that I was fighting a fish! He had plenty of water on either side of us, but he chose to deliberately cut my line, and that tarpon may have been my personal best!"

They watched as the plane taxied over in the direction of the house on Metompkin Island.

"Pull up the trolling motor, Rik; I have a few things I want to say to that guy."

Casey started the outboard and brought the boat up to a fast idle, matching speed with the seaplane as they crossed the little bay. As the plane pulled up beside the dock, the rear door opened, and the same guy who had tied it up at the Bluffs repeated the procedure. He was quickly joined on the dock by the pilot as Casey and Rikki pulled up next to the dock on the opposite side of the plane.

"What the hell! You could see we were there, yet you almost landed on top of us and then deliberately cut our fly line," Casey shouted.

The pilot stared at Casey as a look of recognition came over his face. "You again! If I had wanted to land on you, I could have. Though I didn't come anywhere near your boat, and I don't know anything about your line."

Rikki spoke up. "Like hell! You could see I was fighting a fish, yet you cut as close as you could without hitting us. It was obvious my line was right there and that it wasn't just monofilament. That was a fly line you ruined and will cost over a hundred bucks to replace."

The other guy responded. "Well, if fly fishing is too expensive for you, maybe you should stick to cane poles and bobbers." He smirked and looked at the pilot, who also chuckled.

"And maybe you two jackasses should get in your plane and go back to Miami," Casey said.

That startled the pilot, who was about to respond when his partner nudged him and nodded in the direction of the beach, where two women were now walking toward the house. He told his partner, "Go take care of them."

The pilot refocused his attention on Casey and Rikki, eyeing each suspiciously, knowing now they must've looked up the plane's registration. "As I said, I don't know anything about your line, but I do know this is private property, and you need to leave."

"We're not on your property. We're floating free in navigable water, which is the public domain. And that still doesn't give you the right to land so close to us and cost me that fish and my line!" Rikki wasn't about to calm down anytime soon.

When the pilot had turned to look at the approaching women, his shirt had tightened at the waistline, and Casey had seen the "print" outline of a pistol under it. He moved up beside Rikki, putting a hand on her shoulder in warning. She looked questioningly at him and now saw the serious look on his face.

"Let's go home, Rik. The fishing is ruined here today anyway, and we don't have a spare fly line with us."

The pilot said, "Yeah, go home. I'm tired of you putting your nose in where it doesn't belong."

Rikki was about to say something, but Casey squeezed her arm. He'd not only seen the outline of the gun, but now the second man had intercepted the two women. He'd grabbed both of them by their upper arms and was roughly shoving them over to the stairs. Glancing at him and then where he was looking, Rikki saw how the women were being treated and realized that there was something more happening here. She also knew that Casey didn't normally back away from a fight, and if he was saying they needed to go, it was the better part of wisdom.

Rikki glared at the pilot as she moved back to the rear bench seat with Casey, not saying another word. He started the outboard, backing the boat away from the dock. Casey turned the skiff and set a course around the tip of the sandbar and into the inlet as he brought the boat up to cruising speed. Once out of sight of the house, he slowed back down to idle.

Rikki said, "That was sketchy."

"Yeah. I don't think the two women are regular houseguests."

"Hookers?"

Casey shrugged. "Maybe. The two guys sure didn't look like they were happy about them being out and wandering around. I was trying to warn you that the pilot is carrying."

"Damn! I missed that."

"Something isn't right there," Casey said.

"Agreed. You say he has a pistol, they're roughing up those two women, and they have a seaplane that's outfitted for long-range trips. I'm thinking a call to Stephanie Baker may be in order?"

"My thoughts exactly." Casey took out his cell phone and hit a number on his speed dial. Stephanie Baker was an FBI agent who worked out of the Chesapeake, Virginia, office and a good friend of both of theirs.

Stephanie picked up on the first ring. "I was just about to call our buddy Rikki." Casey had put the call on speaker.

"You don't need to, she's in the boat with me, and you're on speaker."

Rikki asked, "What's up?"

"I need to talk to you about a certain internet search you made last night, but I need to do it in person."

"How did you... well... I only researched one thing last night, and that's part of what we were calling you about."

"Don't say any more on the phone. Where are you guys?"

Casey replied, "Off Cedar Island, heading for the Bluffs."

"I'm twenty minutes away, and I'll meet you there." Stephanie hung up, leaving Casey and Rikki staring at one another, wondering what hornet's nest they'd just kicked.

22

Rella and Harper were both out of breath. Between their reconnaissance walk and Apollo's rough handling of them into the house, they both felt every bruise and scrape the past thirty-six hours had delivered.

"Make yourself at home," Harper said to Apollo as he stomped inside, flashing her hand around.

Rella gave her a *stop it* look and turned on Apollo, who banged the door closed. "The threats stop here and now. I'm ready to hold up my end of the deal and transfer the money. When will we be going to the bank?"

Apollo grunted as he looked around, noticing the rearranged furniture. "There has been a change in plans. Have a seat." He pointed to the floor. "I'll let Zeus share the news."

"Go f—"

Rella grabbed Harper's arm, cutting her off. The two pushed the couch back from the chairs and then arranged them to face one another with several feet between them. "If you're planning on spending the night, there's no other furniture in the house, but then I suppose you know that." Rella plunked down on the couch, Harper next to her.

"Thought you were bringing food." Harper eyed Apollo like the rodent that the two thought he was.

"Stop," Rella mouthed.

"You're S-O-L." Apollo ground his teeth.

"You too, unless you're a canned food lover." Harper flashed a phony smile.

Rella nudged Harper as the last thing she wanted was for her friend to get shot when they were this close to... who knows what.

Apollo stomped to the front door, threw it open, and went out to the railing.

"Don't push him over the edge," Rella told Harper. "Either one of them."

"I know you haven't lost hope that we're getting out of here, but I have. I don't think we're going anywhere. Do they leave us alive or feed us to the fish?"

"Don't give up yet. I've got what they want, and they don't have it. They didn't go this far to leave forty-nine million on the table. Something chased them out of the Caymans, and I have to wonder if it has anything to do with the million I already transferred. I will use every trick our computer guy taught me to buy us time and hopefully our freedom."

"We both need to ensure he's rewarded generously if it's his talents that get us out of here." Harper leaned her head on Rella's shoulder. "I also heard *behave* behind your words, and I will. You're about to see 'get along, Harper.'"

Rella watched as Apollo stepped back and stood in the doorway, poking his head inside. He hadn't paid one bit of attention to the two women, or he'd be harping that they not speak. Footsteps could be heard coming up the steps and stomping across the deck. Apollo then joined Zeus at the railing, and the two were in intense conversation, their eyes peeled to the water.

Harper craned her neck. "Zeus has got a briefcase. If there's a laptop in it, good luck getting it to work based on what I saw as we walked up the beach. This house is powered by solar and, judging by the lighting in this place, not working well."

"It's not good news if he did bring a laptop, as it would mean we're not going anywhere."

The two men could now be heard yelling back and forth.

"Let's hope they're not arguing over whether to cut their losses and just kill us." Harper grimaced. "Apollo would choose something gruesome and risk painting the sand with red. He'd be stupid to do it in here—but then he's not the smartest."

The two men tromped into the house. Zeus looked around suspiciously, no doubt wondering what his captives had been up to. He checked out the rest of the tiny house, and within thirty seconds, appearing appeased, he returned to the kitchen. "Get in here," he yelled.

Rella and Harper exchanged raised eyebrows and stood.

"He means you." Apollo pointed to Rella. "Your friend sits her butt back down."

Rella hooked her arm through Harper's before she could sit back down. "I'm not going anywhere without her."

Apollo smirked. *You'll find out you don't have the upper hand.* He didn't utter another word about Harper staying seated.

Rella led the way to the kitchen, and since there was no place to sit, stood at the end of the counter, waiting to see what happened next. Harper leaned up against the empty pantry cupboard.

Zeus set his briefcase down, opened it, and pulled out a small black box and a laptop.

"Portable Wi-Fi?" Rella asked.

Zeus snorted. "It's an internet satellite link."

"You expect me to make a multi-million-dollar transfer

over that?" Rella asked, eye roll in her tone. She really wanted to tell him *never going to happen no matter what electronics you produce.*

"State of the art," he said as he set it up.

"Once the transfers go through, and then what?" Rella asked. "I have an offer that you two should think about. Take me to the nearest bank, and I'll fill your briefcase with cash, and then you can disappear. You could be in another country in a few hours."

"Tempting, but you and I both know that kind of cash would garner a lot of unwanted attention. There's a good chance we wouldn't make it out of the bank up here without the cops showing up, but then you'd like that." Zeus sneered and shoved the laptop at Rella. "Make the transfer." Then he tossed a sheet of paper down.

Rella covered her shock at only seeing one account number. They were in a hurry to get the money and were making big mistakes. She moved at a snail's pace, accessed her account, and sent an alert with every keystroke. She had no doubt that the two men were trying to watch everything she was doing.

"Now that you're logged in," Apollo said excitedly, "we have all your information…"

Zeus growled, imitating an angry pit bull, and Apollo quickly shut up.

Zeus jerked his head, and Apollo stomped across the room, opened the front door, and stood staring outside. Within minutes, he yelled something back to Zeus in the foreign language no one else understood.

"Expecting someone?" Rella played on the paranoia she noticed from the two men, who weren't as calm and collected as they'd been back in the Cayman Islands.

Harper cut into the man's snarl. "Thought I'd make myself some soup. Would you like some?"

"I don't know what you're up to, but knock it off." Zeus snarled.

Rella almost laughed as Harper zipped her lips. She struggled to contain her grin when a message appeared on the screen that she needed to complete the transaction in person at her branch in Miami. "We've got a problem." She turned the laptop around and let Zeus read it for himself. *Due to security concerns, you must come to your branch to complete this transaction.*

He unleashed a litany in that foreign tongue that Rella was certain was every dirty word he knew. His hand slammed down on the lid, moved around her, pulled out his phone, and stomped straight for the door.

Rella turned to Harper, who'd stayed close, and whispered. "The bank sent an interesting message," and told her what the screen said. "Could be legit because of the amount of the transfer. I want to think it's because one of my alerts worked. Or so many stacked on top of one another."

"How often has your foundation transferred money in the millions?"

"Never."

"Thought it was nuts that they wanted to do it online." Harper shook her head. "The fact that they think they're speeding up might have something to do with the fact that both of them have been so jittery since they got back here. Wherever 'here' is?"

"Zeus is over there having an animated conversation with, I'm guessing, the Honcho, as he's got that pinched look. I've seen him sport that one before while on the phone and mostly listening. It's clear he doesn't like being told what to do." Rella said, turning to Harper. "Just guessing, but it probably has something to do with having to make a trip to Miami that they know is risky. News flash: I'm not going anywhere without you."

"Once in Miami, we take any opportunity to get away. Betting we can navigate the streets better than they can." Harper stiffened and took a step back as Zeus returned, closing in on her and Rella, standing way too close.

"We're on our way to Miami," Zeus said, the irritation rolling off him in waves, putting his electronics back in the briefcase. "Your friend stays here."

"Deal's off unless Harper makes the trip with me." Rella returned his stare down. "If you want to keep us separated once we get to Miami—fine."

"Boss," Apollo yelled. "Visitors."

Zeus drew his gun and joined Apollo at the door. The sound of a boat's engine could be heard in the distance, getting closer. After a minute, he said, "It's the same a-holes from before, except there's another woman."

"What do you suppose they want?" Apollo asked.

Rella and Harper had moved into the living room, wanting to know what was happening.

Zeus returned to where Rella and Harper were standing, and like Apollo, he had his gun at his side. "Sit on the couch, and don't move. Say one word out of line, and you'll start a war, and the other three will die before you two."

"Is it too much to hope that this visit has anything to do with us?" Harper lowered her voice as they sat down.

"If it does, don't you think it would start a gunfight?"

"Probably, so we play ball and get back to Miami. They're not going to be able to shoot up the streets there, as too many are armed."

Rella nodded in agreement. They both tried to hear what was being said, but neither could make out a word.

"Rella, honey," Zeus called as he came back inside. "Police

are here to do a welfare check." He lowered his voice. "Time to trot out the performance of a lifetime."

Rella pasted on a practiced smile and got up, as did Harper, who ignored Zeus's glare, and the three of them went to the door. Rella immediately noted that the two women and the man standing in front of her were gunned up. Tempted to yell, "Help," she stopped, knowing it might start a war, with innocents ending up dead.

"I'm FBI Special Agent Baker," one of the women introduced herself and flashed a badge. "We're not used to seeing people here on Metompkin Island and wanted to make sure there weren't any problems here."

"We're here as a guest of the non-profit that bought the island," Zeus stepped in and answered. "You can call and verify it if you wish."

"We thought it would be a fun adventure, but it turned out to be a bit more rustic than we were expecting," Rella said. "It so happens that we're on our way back to Miami."

"If you're certain. So that you know, we're here to help in any way we can." Agent Baker eyed her and Harper intently.

"As Rella said, this was a fun adventure, but we would like a few more amenities." Harper laughed.

"I can understand that," the agent agreed after she'd stuck her head inside the door and looked around.

"We'll all walk down to the dock together," Zeus said amicably, closing the door after Stephanie was back outside.

Reaching the dock, the agent asked, "Did you forget your bags?"

"On board already." Zeus tipped his head in thanks.

It looked as though the agent and her friends wanted to check out the seaplane, but Zeus and Apollo stood between them and the Cessna, blocking them from getting too close. The men stayed put until Rella and Harper climbed on board.

"Did you notice we were the only two without a gun?" Harper asked as the pair sat down. Rella nodded. "Let's hope all that fake smiling shows we've decided to be cooperative and earns us some brownie points."

Zeus and Apollo hustled on board after untying the plane. Zeus started the engine and didn't waste any time getting airborne.

The journey from the Cayman Islands had felt like an eternity, but this trip was shorter and more seamless. There weren't any pitstops for fuel or outhouse breaks. Rella and Harper exchanged skeptical glances as the plane touched down on the water next to a concrete ramp connected to a compact tarmac with another seaplane parked on it. They had expected to land at an airport, not whatever this was. Both the ramp and a small nearby building were suffering from severe neglect. This was an unrecognizable part of Miami that they'd never seen before.

23

Casey backed the skiff away from the dock, and the three of them watched as the Cessna took off. It climbed to a low altitude and set a course that angled slightly offshore but looked like a direct route to Miami.

"I don't care what that Rella woman claimed; something is definitely off with that bunch," Stephanie said. "Casey, take us back to that dock; I want to get a better look inside the house. But you two stay on the boat and keep an eye out just in case they circle back."

When they picked her up at the Bluffs, Stephanie had seen each of them retrieve their handguns from their locked cars, putting them and their concealed holsters inside their waistbands. She knew the two would be safe if she left them on the boat. She also knew from prior experience that both were licensed to carry those firearms and were very good shots as well. Besides, the fewer people she had contaminating the crime scene, the better. If indeed it *was* a crime scene.

Rikki said, "Don't you need a warrant first?"

Stephanie put a cupped hand next to her ear. "Did you just hear that? It sounded like someone yelling for help from inside the house. Exigent circumstances." She winked at Rikki right before she stepped up onto the casting platform.

Rikki handled the bow line as they pulled up. Before Casey could even get the stern tied, Stephanie was already on the dock, and she raced up to the door of the house. She came out a few minutes later, stripping off a pair of nitrile gloves and holding a clear plastic baggie containing a small piece of wrinkled paper. She stepped back onto the boat.

"My mistake. It must've been a laughing seagull that I heard." Another wink. "The place is empty, and by that, I mean *empty*. No beds, dressers, nothing. Just a kitchen table and a couch with two chairs. When that woman said that they wanted 'a few more amenities,' she wasn't kidding. The place leaves a lot to be desired."

Casey pointed to the baggie. "So, what's that?"

Stephanie replied, "Someone appears to have jotted down some notes; a bank's name—First American Gulfstream Bank—along with what looks to be an account number. But I've never heard of this bank before."

Casey said, "I have. Several of my commercial properties down in Southeast Florida were financed by them. They're headquartered in Miami."

Stephanie nodded thoughtfully. "Everything keeps coming up Miami. But other than getting a bad vibe from those two guys and their plane being on a BOLO watch list, we don't have any solid evidence of a crime. We don't even know that this paper or the writing on it is theirs. But just to be on the safe side, I'll have forensics dust it for fingerprints and see if we can't find a match."

Rikki had been listening quietly but now asked Casey, "Do you have anyone at that bank you're close to? Someone that owes you a favor?"

He nodded. "The bank's president, Marco Garcia. A few

years ago, I agreed to take a couple of the bank's repossessed properties off their hands right before an audit. They didn't want those nonperforming albatrosses on their balance sheet for a bank examiner to find to mess up their performing loan ratio. We rushed the closing, and he was thankful that I was willing to do that."

"Think he might be able to tell you who owns this account, assuming that it *is* an account at that bank?"

"Never hurts to ask, and yeah, I think he'll tell me something about it if it is," Casey said.

"Just out of curiosity, Casey, why would you buy a couple of properties that were dogs?" Stephanie asked.

"Because the neighborhood in Boca Raton where they were located was changing, and I knew what could be done to unlock their value and get them paying for themselves quickly. Then I held them for a few years and ended up flipping them for a darn good profit. On one hand, Marco was happy to have let them go. On the other, not so much; he knew what would eventually happen to their value. But it wasn't the bank's job to be a landlord, and it was more important for him to clean up his books ASAP. Plus, I was already a good customer."

"Nice. Okay, let's get back to the Bluffs so I can pick up my car and get back to the office. I need to get this note to forensics and reply to the agency that put out the BOLO on that seaplane."

Stephanie took off for Chesapeake as soon as they got to the dock, and Casey put the skiff back on the lift. Rikki and Casey then drove over to Bayside. Both of their companies had offices adjacent to each other in a one-story building across the circular driveway from the resort's hotel. The two went into

Casey's conference room, where he called Marco Garcia and put the call on speaker.

"Casey! Good to hear from you. Have you come to your senses and decided to move back to Florida? I've still got money to lend, and there's no shortage of real estate deals around, as you know all too well! I still can't believe how much you made on those Boca properties I put you into."

"No, Marco, while I still have several properties in Florida, I love living here in Virginia. But I'm always up for a good deal if you hear of one coming up."

"Hah! You always were. So, what can I do for you today, Casey?"

"I was wondering if you could tell me if this was an account at your bank, and if so, who it belongs to?" He rattled off the numbers from a picture he'd taken of the paper. He heard the clacking of a keyboard through the phone as Garcia checked the number.

When Garcia spoke again, his tone had changed from friendly to cautious and almost curt. "Uh, Casey, where did you get this number?"

"Is it an account at your bank, Marco?"

"I can't talk about this over the phone, Casey; I'm sorry."

Casey was taken aback by the comment. "Meaning that you *could* tell me if we were face to face?"

"I'm just saying I can't talk about this right now."

"Over the phone."

"Right. I'm sorry, Casey, I have to go."

After Marco hung up so abruptly, Casey leaned back in his chair and looked across the table at Rikki.

"That was weird," Rikki said. "Your friend seemed almost paranoid; it was as if he thought someone might be listening in on your call. He sure was in a hurry to hang up."

"Yes, he did, and yes, he was. Many banks in Miami back a

few years ago were targeted by the feds with wiretaps because of all the money laundering that was going on. That call almost felt like it had that same kind of vibe."

Rikki nodded. "I think we can assume that it was an account at his bank and one that he's not happy about. Do you think it might be drug-related?"

"Marco would close any account that even had a whiff of being funded with drug money. He's a straight shooter, which is why he wanted those Boca properties off his books; he runs a clean operation. No, there's something else going on here. Maybe it's about whoever owns the account. I just don't get it."

Casey's cell phone rang; he answered on speaker when he saw it was Stephanie calling. "You didn't get a hit on the prints from that paper already, did you?"

"I haven't even gotten to the office yet. But I called and had another agent run the name 'Rella' and got a hit. There's a BOLO out on a Rella Cabot and a Harper Finn who disappeared off a yacht down in Grand Cayman two days ago. Cabot is a big philanthropist and held a fundraiser down there. As part of it, they had an offshore booze cruise where they vanished. He texted me the pictures, and there's no doubt about it; they match the two women on Metompkin."

Rikki whistled, "So they were kidnapped?"

"Looks that way, Rikki. We've alerted the Miami field office, and they're watching the airports for the seaplane. I've been ordered to Miami since I can identify the two men that are apparently holding her. I'm going to book a flight as soon as I get into the office."

Casey spoke up. "Know what's better than one person who can identify them? Three people. Up for a quick trip to Miami, Rik?"

Rikki nodded. "Damn right. I've got a score to settle with those two."

"We'll take my jet. We can be there within three hours and might even beat that seaplane. Up for hitching a ride, Stephanie?"

"Absolutely. Uncle Sam thanks you for saving the government airfare, Casey."

"No worries. Meet us at Hampton Roads Executive Terminal in forty-five minutes. And we'll fill you in on the way down about an interesting conversation that we just had."

24

"Welcome to Miami." Apollo threw up his hands, amusing himself more than anyone else, then herded Rella and Harper out of the plane and into a black two-door sedan.

Apollo moved up the seat and shoved Harper toward the back seat, showing his impatience that neither woman had climbed inside already. Harper elbowed him, and not expecting it, he stumbled back a step.

"You want something? Spit it out,"

she snapped. "Next time, try using your words," she added in a tone implying he was six years old.

Proud of her friend for sticking up for herself, Rella moved up behind Harper as she climbed inside, knowing he wouldn't touch her, and got in after.

Zeus, who'd gotten behind the wheel, revved the engine, and once Apollo was inside, hit the gas and squealed out onto a narrow road. They went over a bridge and onto an unfamiliar street. Without consulting a map or GPS, he made several turns, clearly familiar with the area.

Harper leaned into Rella and whispered, "Where are we?"

Rella shrugged, having the same question. Miami covered a lot of square miles.

Apollo, who had one eye glued to the mirror in the open visor, yelled, "Both of you, shut the hell up."

Zeus made several turns, and every time, the area got seedier.

Rella knew that even if she and Harper *could* get away, there was no way they'd chance sneaking down one of those streets. The attention they'd attract could get them in even worse trouble than they were already in.

Zeus turned onto a street in a run-down neighborhood of apartment buildings separated by vacant land and single-family homes; the lawns turned into parking lots. There wasn't a single person visible anywhere. The area had the vibe of a place where those living there knew everything that went down. He turned into the parking lot of a building surrounded by spiked fencing, for all the good that did, as the gate to block unwanted entry was missing. He parked next to a car that could have used major bodywork repairs.

Apollo jumped out, pushed back the seat, and reached for Harper's arm. She leaned away.

"You need to remember Harper and I are the key to your payday. If you didn't understand, that means don't damage the goods," Rella huffed, and the two women climbed out under their own power.

Whatever silent exchange happened between Apollo and Harper, he growled and drew his gun. "Get moving." He motioned for the women to follow Zeus, then stood back with a grin. "Go ahead and yell; see what that gets you. Nothing. No one will come running. They don't look for trouble around here."

"Let's all calm down," Zeus cautioned, his words dripping insincerity. "We're close to winding everything up."

Rella wondered where her purse had gone. She'd seen it in Zeus's possession once, but that was days ago. He had to know she'd need it to do any business. She linked her arm through Harper's as she surveyed the building. "How about a five-star hotel, and I'll pay?"

Apollo snorted in response.

Zeus shook his head and led the way into the building.

Rella and Harper followed, and as they crossed the threshold, they coughed and covered their noses at the rancid odor, courtesy of the dirt that edged up the concrete walls, dead bugs, and overflowing trash. An "out of order" sign was displayed prominently on the elevator. The door to the stairwell stood open, exposing a dank and murky space.

Harper squeezed Rella's hand.

Zeus whipped out keys, opened the last door down the long hallway, and walked inside. "Don't think being on the ground floor means an easy escape—the windows are all barred."

Apollo closed the door and stood with his back to it, staring at the two women.

Zeus claimed one of the barstools and pointed them to the couch, which was in good shape, all things considered. "As I'm certain you're aware, if you transfer money this late in the day, the bank holds onto it until morning. So we'll be at the bank first thing tomorrow." He nodded to Apollo, and the two men exchanged some kind of silent communication.

Apollo moved to the far end of the couch and stuck his gun in Harper's face. "Get up."

She was halfway to her feet when Rella grabbed the back of her dress and jerked her back down. "What's going on?" Rella demanded.

Zeus tipped his chin at Apollo, who took a half-step back. "Here's the deal: you two are being separated—"

"The hell we are," Rella yelled. "You want my money? My friend stays put or you're not getting squat."

"Calm down. She'll be back in the morning." Zeus appeared to be lying through his tight lips. "It's an assurance you'll both behave. We can do this the easy way or the painful way, and we all know which Apollo prefers."

Harper stood, hugged Rella, and hurriedly whispered, "If I'm not back in the morning and you get a way out, take it."

"Break up the lovey stuff," Zeus ordered.

"Know this, if Harper's a no-show, the deal's off," Rella said with more bravado than she was feeling.

Apollo waved his gun toward the door. "Dare you to run." He cocked it.

Harper exited calmly, which would have worried a halfway sane man.

Rella hated when the door closed, wondering if she'd ever see her friend again. They'd been through a lot already, and she didn't want it to end this way. "Why is it you can't stick to the deal we agreed to? If you had, neither of us would be here right now."

"Then you'd be on the phone to the cops," he sneered.

"Anything happens to us, Harper's husband is a retired police detective turned PI and will hunt you down. You'll die, but it won't be quick." Rella was fairly certain Grey wouldn't break the law, but she wouldn't care if he did, and letting Zeus think he'd be dismembered might get him to change course. Or perhaps that was wishful thinking.

"Stop with the threats. She'll be back in the morning." Zeus picked up the remote, plopping down on the couch and practically on top of her.

Rella scooted over with a growl.

"There's a chair." He pointed. "You can have the bedroom. I'm not going anywhere."

She walked over to the window and stared outside. Between the bars, she saw a walkway that backed up to a wood-slat fence and no one in sight in either direction. She craned her neck and decided it must be a path that ran along the side of the building, linking the front to the back.

She turned back to Zeus and raised her hand.

"What?"

"Can I use the bathroom, or should I just do it here?" Rella inwardly smiled, thinking she'd morphed into Harper for a second.

Zeus jerked his thumb in the direction of the only door.

The bedroom was sparse but clean, as was the rest of the apartment. She took note of the few personal items in the bathroom and wondered if Zeus or Apollo lived there. It would have been stupid to bring them here if it were connected to either of them, knowing that if they let her go, she could bring the cops down on them. She wondered if that meant they were stupid or if she was a dead woman walking. She hurried back to the living room before he came looking for her.

Rella sat in a chair and stared mindlessly at the television. He had on a foreign language movie that kept his attention.

"Up to the third floor." Apollo poked Harper with his gun when they got to the stairwell door.

Without acknowledging that she'd heard him, Harper turned into the stairwell, checking out the faint outline of the stairs and then looking up at the five-watt bulb. She grabbed the railing, ignored the smell, and ran up the stairs, leaving Apollo puffing and panting behind her. She waited for him on the third floor.

Apollo pointed to the right. "Second door." He unlocked it.

He stood back, and Harper walked inside, immediately noticing the silence, as every apartment they'd passed had sounded like it had the television on as loud as it would go. Apollo didn't appear to care if she ran, as he'd re-holstered his gun. She figured she wouldn't get far before he drew it again and put a bullet in her.

Harper noted that the apartment was sparsely decorated and similar to the downstairs unit as she claimed a chair. Another thing the two units had in common—they were clean. She didn't miss the dirt she'd been wallowing in the last few days.

"Surprised that rank smell in the hallway hasn't found its way in here," she said as she looked around. "You could've kept us together; we had no plans to run."

"Who'd believe you?" He shook his head, his eyes on the television. He'd decided on a basketball game.

"Isn't it getting complicated, dragging us from one country to another, onto a deserted island, and now this place?

Apollo turned up the sound on the television.

Surprised he didn't just say "Shut up" and save his hearing, she waved to catch his attention and mimed zipping her lips. Surprisingly, he turned it down. She eventually laid her head back and closed her eyes, blaming fatigue from not having any sleep, or very little anyway, since the day they were kidnapped.

25

After picking up Stephanie, Casey relayed his conversation with Marco Garcia as they climbed up to their cruising altitude. "Marco and I go back several years, and he's never acted like that with me before."

Stephanie said, "When we land, that's our first stop. We should be there shortly before they close. Rikki and I will stay out in the lobby while you go talk to him, one on one. At this point, I don't want to take the time to get a warrant unless we have to, and I don't want to make him nervous and have him clam up. But we need to find out who owns that account and why it has him so hinky."

A Miami FBI field agent, Bob Franks, pulled his car up to the jet as it rolled to a stop. He introduced himself to the trio as they loaded into the car.

"We need to go straight to First American Gulfstream Bank, Franks. We know the plane was heading this way, but we might not have beaten them here," Stephanie said.

Ten minutes later, they pulled up in front of an impressive downtown office tower that bore the bank's name in large letters on the top floor. Everything about it seemed to scream *big money* in a very opulent way, which was exactly what the high rollers in this city expected.

Casey was ushered into Marco Garcia's office. The bank's president looked both surprised as well as apprehensive to see him as he came out from behind his desk and shook his hand. They sat down at Marco's worktable.

"When I said I couldn't talk over the phone, I had no idea you would come down here."

Casey shrugged. "I got the feeling that you would be willing to talk if we were face-to-face. What is it that has you so nervous about this account? I'm assuming that it *is* one of your bank's accounts."

"Uh, well, yes, but there are some federal entanglements that are connected with it, and it has the potential to become a big mess for the bank. Beyond that, I don't know how much I can tell you. How did you come to be, uh, associated with it?"

Marco was now looking at Casey with a more critical eye; his initial warmth upon seeing his old customer now seemed to be cooling by the second. Casey knew he needed to do something to bypass this new "federal entanglements" roadblock.

"The feds are part of why I'm here. I brought FBI Agent Stephanie Baker from their Chesapeake field office down with me. She's waiting in the lobby along with an agent from their Miami field office and a mutual friend who is in the private security business. Would you mind if they joined us?" Casey now figured that bringing the feds into the conversation might make Garcia more at ease.

"No, that would be fine. In fact, that would be a good idea

to have someone from the FBI in with us; then I'll be able to share a bit more with you."

The two stood, then Casey made the introductions when the trio joined them. Marco motioned to three empty chairs at the table.

"I couldn't be too forthcoming with the details about that account with Casey because it is under a watch order by your agency, as you are probably aware," he nodded toward Stephanie and Franks.

Stephanie replied, "No, I don't know about your watch order. The name of your bank and that account number came up in an investigation into a missing persons case. We need to know who owns it and the reason it's being watched."

Garcia looked surprised that the account might be connected to a missing persons case. "It's a commercial account belonging to a yacht sales and charter company that we've dealt with for years. I figured that it was under watch because of the large amounts of money that used to flow through it, some of it coming from and going to offshore accounts. Though with the price of yachts and charters these days, it wasn't unusually high for that kind of account. More and more yacht deals are closed outside of the US in order to avoid taxes now, so we have to wire those funds to offshore banks. Those kinds of transactions move through that account rather than the escrow account that they also have here with us. But this is the first I've heard anything about any missing persons."

Stephanie asked, "You said 'that used to flow through' that account?"

Garcia nodded. "Yes, it wasn't that unusual to have millions of dollars passing through it every month. Their cash flow was part of the reason we financed a new yacht for their company last year and a seaplane for an affiliated company of theirs. But they'd only made a few payments on each before their cash flow dried up. Both companies are now far in arrears on those loans.

"Frankly, I've already had the paperwork drawn up to seize those two assets. We made sure they had the yacht documented as part of the loan agreement. That certification makes it much easier for us to take possession. Then I got a call from the owner this morning. He told me that they were about to have a substantial capital infusion wired into that account either today or tomorrow that would much more than cover the overdue payments.

"I was relieved since I was about to look for a repo agent to execute those papers. I was concerned that the owner might have been running with the assets since the last location on the yacht's automated identification system showed it was in the Cayman Islands. Then it went dark this morning; the unit must've been turned off. But since it's documented by the US Coast Guard, we can grab it while it's down there, *if* it's still down there. Unfortunately, I don't have any idea where the plane is.

"Having each repossessed would cost up to ten percent of their current values, in addition to the carrying costs until each would be able to be sold. It would undoubtedly be less than a wash on the equity in each and could end up costing the bank seven figures if we have to go that route.

"I'd actually thought about calling you Casey if we did since you're a yacht and airplane kind of guy. But it looks like that's going to be a moot point. At least, I hope it will be, but…" Garcia seemed to think better of adding to what he was saying.

"But what, Marco?" Casey asked.

"It's just that the customer wants the remainder of the account after the loans are brought up to date to be paid out in cash after his wire hits here. We're talking far in excess of forty million dollars, and we don't keep that kind of cash on hand. Once it gets credited to the account, we can put in an order with the Federal Reserve Bank to have the cash delivered to us, but that won't happen for another day. That kind of thing used to be common back in the eighties but not so much today."

"Meanwhile, you get the interest on the account overnight by parking it with the Federal Bank," Franks said.

Garcia shrugged. "It's just how things work. However, I neglected to tell my customer about that part. I want the money here in the account first. Then we may decide if we want to go ahead and call those loans in full or require an equal amount to be kept on deposit with us. If that yacht is still in the Caymans, there's no way I'm releasing all that cash."

Rikki asked, "That airplane wouldn't happen to be a turbo-prop Cessna Caravan Amphibian, would it?"

Garcia's eyes narrowed. "Yes, it would. How did you know that?"

"Just a hunch. But if I were you, I think I'd plan on using those repo papers because I'm sure the feds will be seizing all of the money."

Now Garcia's eyes widened. "Drugs?"

Stephanie spoke up. "Rikki is probably right. If I don't miss my guess, that's probably not from drugs but a ransom payment instead. Your Cessna may have been involved in transporting two kidnapped women who disappeared in the Caymans after attending a party on a yacht."

She told Marco the tail number of the plane, and they watched the color drain from his face, silently confirming her suggestion. They could see the wheels turning in his head. If this turned out to be true, his bank could at least be out the cost of the loan as well as the collateral if the plane was seized. Worse, if it turned out that the yacht involved was the one his customer financed through him, that might be at risk as well. The chances were not looking good.

Stephanie said, "Well, it looks like there's nothing further for us to do here today since the bank is already closing for the day. Franks, if you can drop us off at a hotel, we'll come back in the morning. That is if you two are able to stay here overnight." She indicated Rikki and Casey.

"Absolutely. I want to see this through and help those women," Casey said. He looked at Rikki, who nodded in agreement.

"Plus, nobody costs me a fly line and a trophy fish and gets away with it." Rikki had a semi-serious look on her face as she said it, as Franks and Garcia both looked confused.

26

Curled up in the chair across from Zeus, Rella had finally fallen asleep. She opened her eyes, disoriented for a minute. Zeus was barking into his phone, mad about something. She stretched her neck, her whole body riddled with pain. *Today was the day...* at least, she hoped.

"If you're hungry, I had that delivered." Zeus pointed to a bag on the table and a cup next to it, which she presumed to be coffee.

Rella nodded, startled that she'd slept through the opening of the door. As much as she wanted to make a run for it, she wouldn't, as leaving Harper behind was unthinkable. She stretched her legs, picked up the coffee, snapped the lid off, and frowned—it was cold. She took a drink, managed to keep it down, and put the top back on, setting it down and searching in the bag—two glazed donuts. She grabbed both and went back and claimed her chair. "Thank you."

"When you're finished, try to lose the homeless look." Zeus gave her a sneering once-over.

Whose fault is that? Rella mustered a fake smile. "I'll get on it."

Zeus got up and went into the kitchen, phone in hand.

She knew he was making calls, as she could hear him talking, but she couldn't make out a word of what he was saying. She forced herself to stay in the moment, knowing she'd otherwise drive herself crazy, wondering what would happen next. After finishing off one of the donuts, she went into the bathroom, washed her face, and wound her blond mane into a messy bun. It didn't take long, and she was soon seated again, staring mindlessly at the television. Since Zeus hadn't said she couldn't pick a channel, she grabbed the remote and found a news station, keeping the volume low and wondering if she and Harper had made the news. When no report of their kidnapping came up, she was both disappointed and relieved because she knew if they were mentioned, she and Harper wouldn't be walking out of there.

The front door opened, and Harper walked in, followed by Apollo, who was grinding his teeth. Harper hurried in Rella's direction, and though she was sitting in an oversized chair and there wasn't a lot of extra room, the two smooshed together.

"Do you think they're really going to keep their word?" Harper whispered, even though Apollo had headed to the kitchen and the men's voices could be heard.

"Trying not to be a Rella-downer, but let's not get too hopeful until they take us both to the bank," she whispered back. "I've been clear about what they need to do if they want the money."

"Someone called last night and bitched out Apollo. I couldn't hear the particulars, even though he held the phone away from his ear due to the shouting, and when Apollo hung up, he was ready to spit nails. I think he wanted to take his frustration out on me, but I closed my eyes and pretended to sleep," Harper confided.

"I know you'd rather beat the snuff out of him, but I'm happy you didn't try to go that route."

"You know me so well." Harper got up, and grabbed the coffee and donut from where Rella had left it. She went back to her chair and dropped the latter in her lap.

As Harper removed the coffee lid, Rella warned, "It's cold and tastes like…" She made a face.

Harper took a sniff, passed, then turned her attention to the donut and took a bite. "Beats starving," she said between bites. "Can't believe you got a gourmet meal, and I got nothing."

"What are you talking about?" Zeus snapped, coming back into the living room, Apollo behind him.

"Just telling Rella how impressive it was of you to buy something akin to dog food for breakfast." Harper grinned at him.

Not amused, Zeus's jaw tightened. "Get up and keep your mouths shut."

Rella put her hand on Harper's leg. "Not to be contrary, but can you tell us where we're going?"

"The bank," Zeus said as though she was stupid.

"And Harper's coming along?" Rella didn't care if he was irked off. She wanted assurances and reminded herself there was no guarantee of him keeping his word.

"You're getting what you want," he seethed in disgust.

Rella jumped up, held out her hand to Harper, and the two headed out the door Apollo had opened. He led the way to the car, an SUV they hadn't seen before. Two men leaned against the bumper, smoking and checking them out. They nodded at Apollo and took off.

"Guess this vehicle wasn't stolen because they paid for protection," Harper said, climbing in.

Rella, right behind her, said, "This pep talk is for both of us: Behave. Don't give them a reason to go off the rails."

"Move over," Apollo grouched, sliding in the back and sitting beside them.

It was a silent ride as Zeus maneuvered through side roads to the foundation's bank. Once there, he bypassed the underground parking and found a space on the street a couple of blocks away.

"Okay, you two." Zeus turned in his seat, staring them down. "We're going to partner up." He pointed to Rella. "You and Apollo will make the transfer. Harper and I will stay in the car. Think of it as insurance against you doing something stupid. Then the four of us will part ways soon if all goes as planned."

Rella was surprised that Zeus left the threats implied for a change. She got out, joining Apollo on the sidewalk. He reached for her arm, but she shook his hand off. "No need to be all touchy, as we're not deviating from the plan," Rella said, walking at his side.

The two of them went up a set of spiral stairs into the bank building, one in a line of tall and impressive office towers. Apollo opened the lobby door, and he escorted Rella over to the bank. Once inside, she signed in like any other customer, and they both took a seat.

It wasn't long before the bank manager stood in front of them, introducing herself to Apollo as Ashley Davis and greeting Rella like an old friend. The two other customers already waiting in the lobby glared as Rella and Apollo were escorted into the office. Once in the office, they all took a seat.

"How can I help you today, Ms. Cabot?"

"I need to make a transfer," Rella said. Not wanting anyone to get hurt, she made it sound like business as usual.

The manager brought up the paperwork on her computer screen, and Rella gave her the account information. When she stated the amount of the transfer, Ms. Davis's shock was evident. She entered the data and pushed a keypad at Rella, who entered a password that should have triggered an alert, then continued with the transfer.

Ms. Davis handed her the receipt. "All finished. Is there anything else that I can help you with today?"

Apollo answered before Rella could say anything. "No, we're good. Let's go, Rella." He ushered her out of the bank and down the street to the car, where he shoved her roughly into the back seat.

"Hey! This was not our deal... I transferred the money. Now let us go!"

"First, we go to our bank to make sure that transfer really got there. If it did, then we'll cut you loose."

Five minutes later, after pulling up in front of First American Gulfstream Bank, Zeus turned and said, "Now, both of you stay here and keep me company while Apollo goes in and handles our business. Keep quiet until he gets back, and you better pray that money is here."

27

Garcia's phone buzzed, interrupting his train of thought. He picked up and listened, then said, "Send them in." He looked at the others in the room and said, "Someone from the yacht brokerage is here."

A minute later, Apollo walked in. He didn't make it three steps past the door before he spotted Stephanie, Casey, and Rikki, then stopped dead in his tracks. Instantly he was grabbed from behind by Franks and another agent and then wrestled to the floor. Franks relieved him of his handgun while the other agent handcuffed him. Together they hauled him to his feet. He looked bewildered as he looked at Rikki and asked, "Who are you?"

Rikki walked over to him and said, "You don't recognize me all cleaned up? I'm the one you geniuses really shouldn't have cost that fish and fly line."

Stephanie asked, "Where's your partner, Cabot, and Finn?"

Regaining his composure, he glared at her and said simply, "Lawyer."

Franks turned out Apollo's pockets and checked the interior of the large duffel bag he brought in with him, finding all were empty. After not discovering any car keys, he said, "Well, he didn't walk here. I'd bet his partner is waiting outside somewhere in a vehicle."

"Casey, Rikki, and I can identify him. Let's start by checking out the street and the parking garage," Stephanie said.

Along with Franks, the trio walked through the bank, leaving Apollo inside the office in the custody of the other Miami agent. Out in front, Stephanie said, "Casey, you come with me. Rikki, you go with Franks. Everyone stay sharp; we want to surprise this guy before he can shoot any of us or his hostages."

They headed in opposite directions on the sidewalk. Stephanie and Casey hadn't gone a hundred yards before an SUV on the other side of the street squealed its tires as it pulled out of its parking space. But instead of racing away with the traffic, it shot diagonally across the street and slammed hard into the side of a parked car. The back doors opened, and two women bailed out. They held up their hands when they saw Stephanie's gun pointing in their direction.

"I'm Rella Cabot. My friend and I were kidnapped by the guy in the driver's seat!"

But Zeus was in no shape to resist capture, his head having been turned sideways before the airbags went off. After he'd recognized Stephanie and Casey and started racing away, Harper had jammed her forefingers into his eye sockets from behind him, wrenching his head around. The force of the airbags then sent his head flying sideways rather than cushioning his face and torso into the bag. His brain bounced side to side in his skull, dazing him. He only began regaining his senses after he was dragged out of the door by Franks, and then his face was introduced to some rough Miami asphalt.

Rella exclaimed, "YOU three! How did you get here?" She

had just recognized Agent Baker, Casey, and Rikki. "Never mind. His accomplice is in the bank, and he's also got a pistol!"

"Already got it covered, Mrs. Cabot. But we have a ton of questions for you."

28

Casey's jet touched down at Owen Roberts International Airport in Grand Cayman, shortly after 3:00 p.m., with Sam at the controls. He taxied to the FBO where a customs official waited alongside a tall slender man in a pale colored business suit, white shirt, and no tie. As they disembarked, Rikki led the way and they each handed the customs official their passports.

"Detective Whittaker," the second man introduced himself, as he shook hands with each passenger in turn. "It's a pleasure to meet you, Mrs. Cabot and Mrs. Finn," he said, reaching the last two.

The trip to the island had been a whirlwind after the two thugs had been arrested. Agent Stephanie Baker had quickly put a few more pieces of the puzzle together, and once she explained her findings to Casey and Rikki, Casey immediately offered his plane once again. Rella overheard the conversation and offered to pay for the fuel if she could tag along, which Casey adamantly declined. The reimbursement that is. He was more than happy for Rella and Harper to hitch a ride. They had to recover their luggage after all.

Their husbands weren't nearly as keen on the idea of their wives returning to the island they'd just been kidnapped from, but finally relented under Agent Baker's promise to personally protect them.

"Are we ready?" Whittaker asked, as Casey made sure Sam had all he needed to prepare for the return flight and the customs official stamped the last passport.

"What do we need to do?" Casey asked, buttoning up his Guayabera shirt he'd pulled from his clothes stash in the plane.

"We've been waiting on you to arrive," Whittaker replied. "It's a five-minute drive, if you'd all like to come this way."

The group followed the local policeman, who opened the doors of a white SUV marked Royal Cayman Islands Police Service. Once they'd filled the three rows of seats, Whittaker pulled away, winding through the backstreets of the commercial district by the airport.

"It's nice to have a sedate drive through town," Rella quipped. "Our last journey was one I wouldn't like to repeat."

"I apologize we weren't able to apprehend your kidnappers before they reached the seaplane, ma'am. We couldn't risk firing on the plane with you both inside."

"Were you the one pursuing us?" Harper asked, leaning over from the rear seat.

"I was in the vehicle and then the marine unit boat, but I wasn't at the controls of either one, ma'am."

"Please, call us Rella and Harper, Detective," Rella interjected. "We're glad to be back here under better circumstances and in one piece."

"And we'd like to personally thank those who tried to save us, Detective," Harper added. "Starting with you of course. We appreciate your efforts."

Rella recognized the frontage road leading into George Town's waterfront as the detective turned left. After a moment they passed by the tiny fish market and she noticed a man with his arm in a sling, selling his daily catch from the table.

"Thank you. We pride ourselves on having one of the safest islands in the Caribbean so I deeply regret what happened to you both," he said as he slowed and pulled over by a dive shop fronting the Hog Sty Bay harbor. "And you're about to meet one of those officers in just a moment," he added, turning to face the group. "Agent Baker, if you'd please accompany me, I've arranged for the rest of you to observe from the dive shop here. I have two constables inside waiting for you. I must ask you to remain inside until I come and get you."

Rella nodded her assent and nudged Harper, who reluctantly followed suit.

"No problem," Casey agreed.

"Yeah, thanks for letting us be here," Rikki added.

They all got out of the SUV and followed Whittaker inside the dive shop.

"I remember you," Harper blurted when she saw the tall, slim, Scandinavian looking constable.

"This is Constable Sommer," Whittaker said. "It was her keen observation out by the *Kittiwake* wreck that started our investigation. If she hadn't followed up, we never would have even known you'd been kidnapped until your husbands called us the following day."

Rella extended a hand. "It was chasing them from the island here that threw a wrench in their plans and had them scrambling. There's a good chance we owe you our lives."

Harper stepped forward and threw her arms around the tall woman. "If you're ever in Miami, you must let us know."

Nora looked mortified. She detested being the center of

attention, and was definitely not a hugger. She stood as stiff as a board until the pretty lady released her.

"Can we do this, sir?" she said, looking at Whittaker.

He nodded, but couldn't hide a grin. Stephanie followed the detective as he led her and Nora out the door, where they walked to the adjacent concrete dock. The FBI agent let out a low whistle as she looked at the mega yacht moored alongside.

"Do you have the escape routes covered?" she asked.

"As you can see, there aren't too many options," Whittaker replied. "We have a patrol boat staged outside the harbor and several units behind us to cover the dock. We've been watching the boat all day and it appears the crew are ashore, leaving only two people on board."

"Watch out for the captain," Nora said in a low voice. "We questioned him at length but couldn't pin anything on him. He has a rap sheet."

"Good intel, thanks," Stephanie responded, noticing neither of the Caymanian police officers appeared to be armed. "You're not carrying?"

"No," Whittaker explained as they reached the swim step of the yacht. "We have a firearms unit but they're only deployed in extreme situations. Our marine unit is armed and they can be here at a moment's notice. Besides, the boat was searched upon arrival."

Agent Baker touched a hand to her firearm holstered under her jacket. "Thanks for letting me carry, Detective. I'd feel naked without it."

"They won't let me even take the training until I'm twenty-one," Nora grunted.

Stephanie couldn't decide if she was more surprised that she was the only one armed, or that the ice queen who seemed to have the detective's respect, wasn't even twenty-one years old.

"Just remember to only pull it if any of us or the public are placed in danger," Whittaker politely warned the agent. "We have strict rules about that. No firearms maybe discharged unless someone's in direct danger."

"Hello again," came a voice from above, where Blake Decker smiled down at them. "I do hope you're not harassing my captain again, Detective. I'm already late and plan to leave within the hour."

"May we come aboard, Mr. Decker?" Whittaker asked. "I promise we won't keep you long."

Decker waved them up, and Stephanie followed Whittaker up the curved steps on the starboard side. Nora moved to their left and used the matching stairs on the port side. Stephanie gave her a nod of approval.

Once on the salon deck, the boat owner held the sliding glass door open and let them file inside.

"Miss Sommer," he greeted Nora, but she stopped short of entering the salon.

"I'll wait outside," she said and noticed the FBI agent gave her another subtle nod.

Decker shrugged his shoulders and slid the door closed behind him. Nora watched him walk over to where Whittaker and Agent Baker waited next to the large dining table. She couldn't hear the exchange, but Decker quickly became animated, walking back and forth and pointing at the Caymanian detective. When Baker pulled a piece of paper from her jacket, Decker snatched it from her and studied the document.

Nora leaned over the port side and checked the walkway below. Not seeing or hearing any movement, she moved to the starboard side. Still nothing. She walked to the back of the deck and looked down at the broad swim step below. It struck her as odd that the crew were all ashore, but Decker had said they were about to leave. She had no idea how many people it took to crew a boat of this size, and wondered if two were enough.

Which raised the question of where was the captain? Surely Whittaker would have asked Decker to have Hall join them, but a quick glance through the tall windows into the salon verified the captain wasn't with them. On the port side, a set of stairs led to the upper deck, and Nora quietly scaled the steps and looked across the opulent outdoor furniture to the enclosed lounge. There was no one to be seen.

The slider was open, so she slipped inside and walked to the front partition wall where stairs led down on her right and ahead, a pocket door was partially open. She glided it the rest of the way to reveal the pilothouse. The controls were remarkably simple for such a complex system. Two small joysticks maneuvered the boat, but a wide bank of computer screens displayed a dizzying array of gauges, controls, and options.

As Nora stared at the panel, she heard the engines come to life in a low rumble, and a myriad of graphically displayed gauges were set in motion.

"Captain Hall?" Whittaker's voice called out from below, and Nora stepped back through the pocket door to the stairwell.

Below her, Whittaker appeared and was about to say something when she heard another voice.

"Back in the room, Detective," Hall ordered from somewhere unseen.

Nora nodded to her boss, and stepped away from the stairwell.

"About damn time, Jody," she heard Decker say. "I'll take your firearm, Miss Baker."

Perfect, Nora thought, now both the bad guys have guns,

and we have none. She quickly turned her radio volume down to zero and took out her cell phone.

"Check upstairs," Decker ordered. "The blonde one was with them. She stayed outside, but I don't see her anymore."

Nora hit send on her text, then looked around for somewhere to hide as footsteps fell on the stairs. Her only options were the salon and the exit door to the walkway along the port side, both of which could be seen by anyone coming up the stairs. She stepped to the edge of the doorway and pulled her Taser from her belt.

A hand holding a gun arrived in view first, and she didn't wait to see the rest of the man. Swinging above the gun, she hit Hall in the chest with the Taser and heard him yelp as the gun went off in a deafening report. Nora watched Hall tumble backward down the stairs while pebbles of tempered glass showered down from the window shattered by the errant bullet.

Hall's twitching body thudded to the floor at the base of the stairs and Nora scurried down after him, chasing the gun that had flung from his limp hand, clattering behind him down the polished wood steps. From the salon she heard someone shout and another gunshot went off.

With her eyes locked on the firearm, Nora arrived at the bottom step, just as a hand snatched up the gun before she could reach it. She tried to stop, but her momentum sent her careening into the wall at the bottom of the stairwell while stomping on Hall's contorted body. Before she could recover, an arm was wrapped around her, and a gun pressed to her cheek.

"Drop it!" Decker yelled, holding Nora as a shield before him.

Nora looked into the salon, where Whittaker was picking

himself up from the floor and Agent Baker stood with her own gun she'd recovered, aimed at what felt to Nora like her head.

"Drop the gun, or I'll shoot her," Decker reiterated, his voice shaking.

He had a firm hold around Nora and she could feel his whole body tensed like a wire about to snap. She looked over at Baker.

"Let's all calm down and figure this out," the agent said.

"Drop the fucking gun!" Decker barked. "That's how we'll figure this out."

Nora looked Agent Baker in the eyes. "I'm in direct danger," she said, and gave her a subtle nod.

"What…" Decker began, but Nora swung them both to her left as she dug her Taser into his thigh and revealed the right side of Decker's head which exploded as Baker's shot hit him in the temple.

Nora felt the man's body instantly go limp, falling away from her as the force of the bullet hitting his skull rolled him backward, collapsing atop his captain who gasped at the impact. Nora wiped blood from the side of her face, reached down and emptied the last of her Taser's charge into Captain Hall.

"*Drittsekker*," she muttered, and turned to face Agent Baker.

"That was ballsy," Stephanie said with a relieved smile, holstering her gun.

"Good shot," Nora replied, streaking her shirt sleeve crimson as she continued trying to clean her face.

Whittaker collected Hall's gun from where it fell from Decker's hand to the carpeted salon floor, now splattered in the man's blood. "Constable Sommer creates a lot of paperwork in her wake," he said, resting a hand on Nora's shoulder.

"But that's not the first time she's helped save lives. Good work, both of you."

"On behalf of the FBI, I thank *you* both. You've helped bring these two US criminals to justice, as well as the other two in Miami," Stephanie added.

EPILOGUE

Two days later…

Aboard the *DSTP*, preparations for the return to Miami were in full swing, and Captain Frank Cunningham assured Casey, they'd be ready to depart that afternoon. Two of the captain's mates from *Lady Dawn*, Casey and Dawn's yacht, which also served as their floating home, had flown down with him to deliver the yacht to Miami, where Rikki would turn it over to the bank. In the whirlwind before Rikki had flown down to Grand Cayman, she had cut a deal with Marco Garcia for her security company to act as the bank's agent in repossessing both the plane and the yacht. But instead of cash for her ten percent fee, she offered to settle for the title to the seaplane, which was about equal in value.

"Nice of you two to let us tag along after all on your Cayman vacation," Dawn said slightly sarcastically. She looked over at Cindy, who nodded and smiled in agreement. They had both flown down with the crew to join their significant others as a kind of repayment for having originally been left behind. The four were sitting around the table on the aft part of the skydeck, relaxing and enjoying the sunshine.

Cindy said, "Nice to have had a day 'playing tourist' on the island while all the paperwork was being done."

"Frank and the guys had to lay in provisions for the trip anyway," Casey said. "And make a temporary repair to the glass in the pilothouse."

"I daresay the carpet needed cleaning in the salon as well," Stephanie chimed in, climbing the steps to join them.

The group stood and warmly greeted their friend, as well as Rella and Harper who were with the agent. Casey had held his plane for Sam to fly them all to Miami, along with Joseph Hall, who would of course be in handcuffs.

The new arrivals took a seat, and were quickly handed rum punches, which only Stephanie declined. She was still on duty.

"We're all here," Rikki noted. "It's a shame the detective and Nora couldn't join us."

"We made sure to thank them both," Rella said. "They really put our rescue in motion. I don't think we would have been taken to Metompkin if the police here hadn't gotten so close. From what Whittaker told us, that was all Nora after she saw Harper being taken from the party."

"That girl has ice in her veins," Stephanie said with a smirk. "But let me tell you, Whittaker's no slouch either. If he hadn't knocked my gun out of Decker's hand when Nora started the commotion, things would have probably gone down differently."

Rella stood, and took the opportunity to raise a glass to the group at the table who'd gone above and beyond anyone's expectations to save her and her friend, Harper. Casey, Rikki, and Stephanie waved her off, but they all felt a sense of pride for the role they'd played.

"Hopefully we'll be seeing you back in Virginia soon,"

Casey said to Stephanie as they relaxed and enjoyed their drinks. "You'll be the rock star back at your field office after taking down the head of that kidnapping ring."

"And a former smuggling ringleader," Rikki added.

"What was the deal with that?" Dawn asked.

Stephanie hesitated a moment, as it was an open case, then decided everyone at the table had a right to know. "Decker was running drugs in the seaplane. Fentanyl, cocaine, and counterfeit opioid pills. The yacht brokerage was a great cover and made it easy to wash the profits. But then he lost his supplier, and he was in a cash crunch after buying the Azimut. When you came to him," she continued, looking at Rella, "wanting to charter a yacht in the Caymans, rather than hire one of the local ones, he sent *DSTP* down. It gave him a legitimate reason to have it leave the US while being so far behind on the payments.

"He never intended on the boat, or himself, ever returning to the States, which is why he turned off the positioning transponder after the charter. He only made the outstanding payments to temporarily keep the bank off his back. The seaplane was going to be flown down after all the Miami banking was finished, along with Rella's cash. They probably would've been taken to somewhere in South America, well out of the bank's reach."

"But isn't the FBI going to seize this yacht and the plane?" Dawn asked.

Rikki grinned and Stephanie let her answer the question. "They could have if Decker still had possession of them in the US, but I slapped the repo stickers on the plane before we left, and now I've put them on the side of *DSTP*'s cabin. They officially belong to the bank. The kidnapping technically took place in the Caymans, outside of the FBI's reach. And there was no ongoing smuggling operation nor any evidence to tie Alessandro Roland and Robert Anderson to that."

"Although we're sure they were involved," Stephanie added.

"Who are we talking about?" Rella asked.

"The men you knew as Zeus and Apollo," Stephanie clarified.

"Dumbest codenames ever," Harper chimed in, to which everyone added their agreement.

"They're going down for their part in the kidnapping," Stephanie continued, "and the captain for conspiracy back in the US, as well as assault on a federal officer. Decker was a big donor to that land conservancy group, and was the one who had reserved the cabin on Metompkin. With plenty of evidence about the kidnapping scheme back in the US, the Cayman police were happy to turn him over to me. They didn't want a trial there with all the accompanying negative publicity affecting their tourism."

"But, Rikki, how did you get the repo contract?" Dawn asked.

"Casey helped. It didn't matter to Garcia who repossessed the bank's property, though finding someone else to get it out of the Caymans would've been tough. Stephanie helped grease the wheels with the local authorities to get the yacht released, which was a point in my favor. Garcia realized what Decker intended to do, so he wanted it grabbed ASAP."

Casey tilted his head slightly. "So, you're now a seaplane owner, but you don't fly. What are you going to do with it?"

"I've been meaning to talk to you about that. Sam has been bugging you to add a seaplane to your charter service. Think you might be interested in trading some shares in that company for the Cessna?"

Casey shook his head. "Nope."

Rikki looked shocked as well as disappointed.

He grinned. "No, but I would be willing to trade some shares as well as a new fly line and another day of tarpon fishing. I think that's only fair."

She smiled widely. "Then I'll take your definition of fair, pal!"

"We must be off," Stephanie said, checking a text on her phone. "Detective Whittaker has my prisoner ready to go."

"We have a couple of husbands who are ready for us to come home too, so thank you all again for everything," Rella enthused. "And you all have my direct number if there's ever anything I can do for any of you."

With another round of hugs and salutations, the three ladies made their exit and walked down the dock alongside the impressive mega yacht. Halfway down, Harper paused for a moment, and Rella stopped with her, leaving Agent Baker to continue ahead.

"Everything okay?" Rella asked, resting a hand on her friend's arm.

"I was just thinking," Harper said softly. "Of all the crazy adventures we've been on, and the mountains of trouble we've got ourselves into, this might just take the cake."

Rella reflected on the past handful of days and had to agree. "There were a few times I really didn't think we'd make it home."

Harper shook her head. "I was ready to give up and do something crazy, but you always had hope, and never gave up on me. You risked fifty million dollars because they threatened to hurt me. That's truly unbelievable."

Rella put her arms around her friend and held her close. "That's because you're priceless to me," she whispered. "Priceless."

If you enjoyed *Priceless*, you'll love *Faceless*,
the full-length novel by four more Tropical Authors.

Discover more books in the genre, and sign up for the
newsletter with new releases and great deals at
www.TropicalAuthors.com

ABOUT THE AUTHOR

Deborah Brown is an award-winning author. She writes humorous mysteries set in the Florida Keys. The perfect read for the beach or in front of the fireplace. The Gulf of Mexico is her home, which she shares with two ungrateful rescue cats, and where Mother Nature takes out her bad attitude in the form of hurricanes.

Author of the Florida Keys Mystery Series and the Biscayne Bay Mystery Series.
For more information and to join his newsletter visit his website at DeborahBrownBooks.com.

ABOUT THE AUTHOR

A *USA Today* Bestselling author, Nicholas Harvey's life has been anything but ordinary. Race car driver, adventurer, dive-master, and since 2020, a full-time novelist. Raised in England, Nick has dual US and British citizenship and now lives wherever he and his amazing wife, Cheryl, park their motorhome, or an aeroplane takes them. Warm oceans and tall mountains are their favourite places.

Author of the AJ Bailey Adventure Series and the Nora Sommer Caribbean Suspense Series.
For more information and to join his newsletter, visit his website at HarveyBooks.com.

ABOUT THE AUTHOR

Don Rich is the author of over a dozen bestselling books in the Coastal Beginnings and Coastal Adventure series. His books are set mainly in the mid-Atlantic, mostly because of his love for this great stretch of America's coastline. A fifth-generation Florida native who grew up on the water, he has spent a good portion of his life on, in, under, or beside it. He now makes his home in Central Virginia. When he's not writing or scouting marinas and boatyards for his next story idea, he can often be found on the Chesapeake Bay or the Atlantic Ocean with a fishing rod, throttle, or sailboat tiller in his hand.

Author of the Coastal Adventure Series and the Coastal Beginnings Series.
For more information and to join his newsletter, visit his website at DonRichBooks.com.

Made in the USA
Las Vegas, NV
25 June 2023

73898468R00111